THIRDS

AN *INKED* NOVELLA

NEW YORK TIMES BESTSELLING AUTHOR

STEPHANIE TYLER

WRITING AS

SE JAKES

THIRDS

INKED 2

For Aleks, the third time wasn't the charm...
and fighting for survival was only the beginning...

Aleks is a tattoo artist at Inked. He's also a man with a troubled history and a future bent on vengeance. But his plans for revenge are derailed when he meets a man with ties to his past. A man who also holds a promise of the future.

Brogan is dangerous for Aleks in more ways than one. He's former military, a successful businessman and a strong hand in the bedroom—everything Aleks wants, under the worst possible circumstances. It's up to Aleks to figure out what—and who—is worth fighting for.

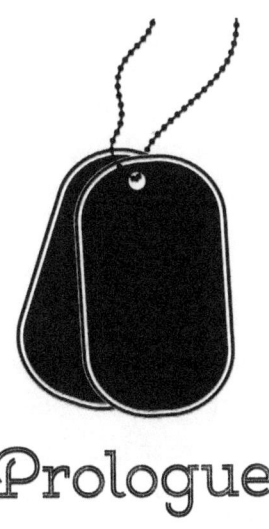

Prologue

EIGHT YEARS EARLIER

Whoever said fucking and fighting were two sides of the same coin must've been a motherfucking virgin.

Last night, I fought the man in front of me, cursing right back at him in Russian in between punishing blows from my fists, the same way I punched the plaster walls in my cells daily, for hours at a time, to numb them, to toughen them up. My fingers had been broken and healed slightly off-center, like the path my life had taken.

I'd take fucking over fighting any day, and yeah, I was damned good at both.

The latter had been exploited for the past twenty-three months, but the end was finally in sight. I'd reached the final stage, the famed deathmatches—and yes, they were exactly what they sounded like. Which was why I strangled the man I'd been punching into unconsciousness, dropped him to the mat as the crowd roared before I was escorted back to my cage.

During my time in this hellhole, I'd been moved from cage to cage to cage. The one I slept in was smaller than the one I trained in, but the one I fought in made me the most claustrophobic.

And the smells—I'd never forget the fucking smells from this place. It was blood and sweat, fear and death combined, and the metallic taste would never leave my mouth. I was sure of it. Still, I'd swish the cold water in my mouth, spit it out between my front teeth in a futile attempt to get rid of it.

But the taste of dread on my tongue lingered, a taunt. A promise. A prayer.

"We're doing this, Aleks," Vann would murmur to me through the bars to keep me going. "No matter what, we're out."

We'd been cellmates for since we'd been voluntarily locked inside this hellhole. No one would rescue us because no one knew we needed rescuing.

That was both a blessing and a curse.

Now, for the third night in a row I was escorted out of my sleeping cell and put into a holding one to watch the third round of deathmatches before mine. I pretended I didn't give a shit that I was watching Vann fight someone to the death, like I wouldn't care one way or another if he died. But inside, my gut twisted, brain screamed at him to *fucking kill the bastard* in front of him.

And he did, dropped the man's lifeless body to the mat and turned to face the crowd, bared his teeth, spit blood on them, hating them and everything about them.

They cheered because they thought he was putting on a show. But they knew—they all knew what was happening and I vowed I'd make them all pay, in the most ruthless and bloody way I knew how.

But first I had to get the fuck out of here. And it was my turn to make that happen. The guy in front of me in the caged ring was my age—eighteen years old. He'd been here the same amount of time, watching fighters like us come and go, mostly in body bags, and he wasn't prepared to die tonight.

Neither was I.

After a few rounds of exchanging blows, I lost it. I wasn't putting on a show for the rich fuckers who paid money to watch me like a monkey in a zoo. I slammed my opponent's face, over and over until his features were unrecognizable, the damage I did to him registering in my gut. But he wasn't as important as the life I was saving, and it sure as hell wasn't mine.

I'd just ended him in the fastest, most humane way I could when I smelled the stench of something burning. My eyes scanned the crowd, which had blurred, although I could sense their panic.

Fire.

The smoke filled my lungs and I wanted to scream, rage, but a strong hand grabbed my wrist.

Vann's voice. "Nothing we can do now but live or die."

Then he tugged and I made the choice along with him to get the hell out of there, into the city streets and cool air and no cages in sight.

I was eighteen years old and, for the first time in two years, I was free.

I had nothing but death to show for it.

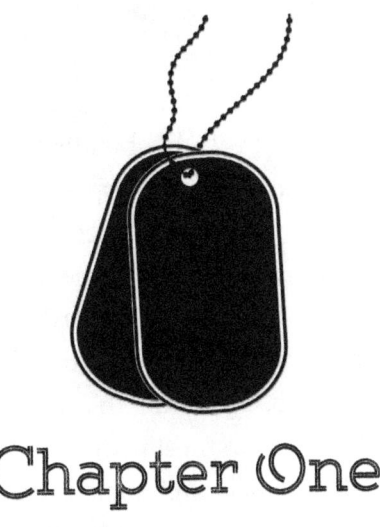

Chapter One

Brogan was finally back home from his extended European stay—six months when he'd only meant to hang out with some friends for a couple of months—and decided to catch up on his real estate holdings. He was lucky enough to have the wealth and a family name behind him that allowed him to travel the way he did, but he also continued to work from abroad.

Brogan preferred the real estate market, with its highs and lows, to the banality of the canning factories and the like that his great-grandfather had established. Without them, there would be no Montgomery-Johnstone money to invest. Because of it, Brogan was able to make himself wealthier.

Still, he sat on the board of directors, the monthly meetings with his cousin Harry and the other men in suits always an experience he wished he didn't have to repeat. Although he'd grown up with Harry, the distance between them couldn't be more apparent.

He had managers and landlords handling the properties, but he liked to keep up with his buildings in person when he could, in case there were any complaints he could rectify. He'd discovered that most people were more reasonable if they thought they were tugging an owner's ear.

He was also a good landlord, and he'd saved his favorite shop for last, a tattoo parlor called Inked. When the building manager originally brought him the lease from the new clients, Brogan had gone to meet with them. One of the men was military, both had solid credit and Brogan knew a good tattoo parlor fit the neighborhood perfectly.

It turned out his hunch was more than right. Each year, the tattoo shop was featured in papers and online for its gifted artists, many of them visiting, since Quinn brought in the artists who'd done his tattoos.

Today, when Brogan pushed open the glass doors, everyone looked over…except the dark-haired man giving a tattoo in the center of the large room.

"Brogan, good to see you again." Quinn, co-owner of the shop and a master tattooer himself came over, hand extended.

"Welcome back, man." Con, his partner—in business and life—came up next and punched him in the shoulder. Quinn's father and brother had served, and Con was former military like Brogan, and he was more than happy to be renting to other vets. They were great tenants, and they were renting the majority of the building out, since Con decided that he also wanted the apartments above the shop so he wouldn't have to, in his words, "commute."

As Brogan got to know them, he quickly realized that although Quinn would often roll his eyes at Con, he also gave in to most of his whims. If Brogan could find someone to make him a quarter as happy, he'd be more than fine with that. "Thanks. Sorry I was gone so long. I'm assuming everything's okay over here?"

"More than," Quinn assured him. "We're still taking bets on when you'll get your first ink."

"Sorry, still not my thing." Brogan's eyes flicked to the man in the shop who most definitely *was*. "You've gotten some fresh faces in here."

"Yeah, we took on a couple of new artists. Becca does piercings and Aleks over there does fantastic pieces." Quinn motioned to the man Brogan had noticed.

Aleks's head had been down as he concentrated. It still was but he raised his chin a bit, enough to make Brogan start.

Because it was *him*, the fighter Brogan had been picturing for what seemed like forever. The image of his sweat-slicked body had gotten Brogan through the worst of Special Forces training, the small piece of comfort he'd allowed himself in those few moments of stolen downtime. He'd used the fighter's image to motivate him, to turn him on, to prove he was still alive when he felt dead inside.

10 YEARS EARLIER

"Gotta show you a good time before you head back into hell," his cousin, Harry, had told him, then ushered him into an underground basement.

This was so far from the good time Brogan planned on having for himself later, in another type of club in another part of the city, but for now, he humored his cousin. Harry liked to act the part of the big spender, which was lost on Brogan, since they shared the same family fortune.

Harry thought Brogan was slumming it in the military. Thought he was crazy to put himself through the gauntlet of Special Forces training, but Brogan could never have done the fraternity shit that he'd been hearing Harry brag about for years.

"We're here for the first fight of the night." Harry handed him a cold beer and pointed to the ring inside the steel cage. The crowd surrounded it, standing outside the chain link as though watching some kind of exotic animals through the metal.

The first guy was shoved into the ring and looked back at the man who'd pushed him out there. He was big and the jeers from he crowd had him giving everyone his middle finger and sneering.

Great. A bunch of overgrown college kids trying to pay their way through school, according to Harry.

But Brogan soon forgot about not wanting to be there when the first guy walked into the ring, escorted by his coach, and was locked inside with an ominously loud clink of a lock clicking into place.

No way out. *Brogan's skin itched as though he was the one trapped.*

The guy had dark hair and hypnotically dark eyes. He scanned the crowd, wearing only blue shorts and white tape on his hands.

"Money on the fighter in blue," his cousin told the man who came around to collect the bets.

"He's favored," the man confirmed, handed them their chits.

Yeah, I favor him.

When the fight began Aleks moved like a blur—fast, slick with sweat and yeah, Brogan had his jack-off material for a good while. The other men in his bunk would be thinking about breasts and Brogan would be dreaming about bringing this fighter to his knees, putting his cock in his mouth, watching him submit.

And now, his fantasy was in front of him, alive and well and tattooing a barrel-chested men on his wide biceps. Concentrating fully on the picture taking shape under his gun, the black and gray ink he constantly wiped away revealing a perfect symbol, a cross with a military insignia above it, an intricate, original design.

Damn, the guy still looked the same. Better, actually. His face was chiseled and matured—model material—his body still muscled but a fighter's muscles.

Aleks didn't have the tattoos back then that Brogan noted running down his arms—he'd only worn blue shorts, so Brogan would've seen them if he had.

Con clapped him on the shoulder and prompted, "Sure you're not in the market for a tattoo?"

Con's brow arched and there was no mistaking his intention. Everyone noticed the way Brogan watched Aleks... except maybe Aleks himself. "I'm in the market, but not for one of my own," Brogan told him.

Con smiled broadly. "Brogan, I like the way you think."

"That's seriously perfect," the Army vet in Aleks's chair

breathed as he stared at the complicated 82nd Airborne symbol on his biceps. It was shaded black and gray with a 3-D look to it. Aleks had helped him pick the perfect spot to highlight it best, using the natural shape of his muscle.

"Looks good on you," Aleks confirmed.

"You serve?"

"No. One of the guys who owns this place did," Aleks said. "I just have the respect and appreciation."

"It shows." The vet shook his hand and gave Aleks the once-over. "I'll be back for another one soon, I'm sure."

"I'll be here," Aleks told him.

The vet glanced back at Aleks as he walked away and Aleks moved to clean his equipment. Tattooing—and being tattooed—was a personal thing, a vulnerable thing, and a lot of times feelings and emotions came out that weren't necessarily the person's true feelings.

This customer's reaction was a product of that—he was straight, Aleks knew, but sometimes after sitting in a chair and getting close the way they had…well, things could feel different. Because of that, Aleks got hit on a lot—men and women alike, young and old. He just seemed to have a magnetic pull. At least that's what lovers had told him.

Probably because he was unavailable. His life was devoted to two things: tattooing and taking down the man who'd ruined both his life and Vann's.

Vann had exacted his own revenge on both their accounts, and he'd found a way back. Aleks was happy for him. He knew he'd never get that far if he didn't exact his own revenge. He stayed up nights, planning. Waiting. And the perfect opportunity would present itself, where the guy wouldn't be surrounded by bodyguards. It was only a matter of time.

But when Brogan Montgomery-Johnstone walked into the tattoo parlor, Aleks was so fucking unprepared, he didn't know if he should walk out the back door or right up into Brogan's face. Because time? It might be up.

He looked just like Aleks remembered—a little older. Tanned. Blond, blue-eyed, All-American and handsome as fuck. His bearing was military and if Aleks closed his eyes, he could picture that night, making fast work of one of his first opponents in the ring while Brogan watched him intently.

Sometimes the fights made Aleks hard—a purely physical reaction his body had to fighting—but that night, it had been all about Brogan's intense stare. If Aleks hadn't been locked back into his cell afterward, he might've left the cage and gone with Brogan somewhere to get fucked.

Now, Brogan's eyes caught and held his, and yes, Brogan remembered him, let it show for a long moment before putting on his "all business" face again for Aleks's bosses.

Aleks would've been content for Brogan to finish up his talk and leave, but Con put a kink in that plan by calling out, "Hey Aleks, come meet Brogan. He owns the building."

And Aleks couldn't refuse that, so he ambled over to reach out and take Brogan's outstretched hand in his. He wasn't a big believer in the whole "bolt of lightning when you meet the right guy" crap, but hell, a shot of electricity seemed to jolt a current through both of them. For a second, they just stared at each other; probably equal parts shock and lust were unmistakable on his face the way they were on Brogan's.

Even if Aleks hadn't recognized him from the fights, he would've from the pictures he'd found of Brogan's cousin,

Harry. Aka the man Aleks had marked for death. So far, Aleks had been able to rule out Brogan's direct involvement in funding the fight club, barring the fact that he shared the same last name and part of a vast family fortune with Harry.

Harry was a major backer—the biggest fish—in the deathmatches. Rumor had it that Harry was the one who'd come up with the concept. As for the whys? That probably could've broken Aleks more easily than any fight ever had if he allowed himself to dwell on it: for *sport*. Harry was rich, bored, looking for easy entertainment for his wealthy and out-of-town clients.

It was also a front for the Russian mob.

And now Harry's cousin was standing right in front of him, like a package with a bow on top.

Leverage.

"Brogan Montgomery-Johnstone's a big deal in this community," Con told him after Brogan had said goodbye… reluctantly, it seemed to Aleks.

"So I've heard," he said dryly. "Was I supposed to kiss his bare feet when he walked in? Or lick his boots first?"

Con shrugged. "Hell, if you're into that, I'm sure he'd be all right with it." When Aleks narrowed his eyes at him, Con explained, "Rumor has it he's a Dom."

Ah, now *that* made a hell of a lot of sense. His body seemed to want to respond to Brogan with a ferocity Aleks wasn't used to. "I'm not in the market for one."

"Hey, don't knock it if you haven't tried it."

Aleks had tried it. Liked it too, just not enough to have

one permanently attached to him. To many fucking rules, too much *yes sir* and *no sir* for his tastes. He'd watched the scene, didn't mind playing, but any relationship didn't sound great to him. Getting close to anyone wasn't on his to-do list. He had Vann and now Con and Quinn, who were cool and looked after him.

He told Con, "I've got all the entanglements I can handle at the moment."

"Famous last words," Quinn murmured as he came up to claim Con and rescue Aleks.

Quinn guided Con upstairs to their apartment. They really had taken over the majority of the building, and although they lived together it was nice that they had a space to live and a separate place to play, complete with Con's pool table.

"Think I freaked Aleks out?" Con asked, the smirk still on his face.

"Maybe a little. He and Brogan had some serious chemistry going," Quinn said, stretching out his shoulder a little—he'd had a long week of tattooing. "A blind man could've seen it."

Con moved to stand behind him and began to rub his shoulder. "Now it's up to Aleks to do something about it. Nab himself a rich man."

"Right. Just like you found your sugar daddy?" Quinn teased, then groaned as Con hit the right spot.

"No joke—I did," Con snarked, then got serious. "Aleks is quiet. A good guy. Quiet."

"You said that," Quinn pointed out.

"Bears repeating. Quiet equals dangerous. Guy's definitely dangerous."

"To who?"

"Anyone he considers an enemy."

Quinn looked over his shoulder and blinked. "Glad we're not on that list."

Con murmured against his cheek, "I'm definitely not. But don't worry, *daddy*—I'll protect you."

"You definitely need a beating."

Con smiled. "And you're just the man to give it to me. So what are you waiting for?"

Chapter Two

Aleks finished up his last job, simple initials on the inside of a woman's wrist (her kid's, not a lover, because Aleks wouldn't have done it—that was the kiss of death to any and all relationships and he'd been the one doing the cover-ups for people who hadn't listened to his advice) and he left work and walked the two blocks to his own building. He'd left his bike in the lot there so he didn't take up street parking, plus it allowed him to prowl the area and keep an eye on anything that looked irregular.

He'd been on high alert since last year, when Vann had done his part of the job. They'd wanted to leave time in between, which left Aleks maybe too much of it to plot and plan.

Of course, now there was the new wrinkle of Brogan. And dammit, why was he attracted to the guy he might also have to kill? At the very least, he'd have to eliminate Brogan's cousin, which would make for some damned awkward family reunions.

Yeah, his sense of humor had definitely gotten more

twisted.

Speaking of twisted, it was time to check in with Vann. When he locked himself inside his apartment, he dialed the number from the burner phone they used for these conversations, because they'd decided they couldn't be too careful about their pasts...and what they'd done about them.

Vann answered on the first ring. "Cool?"

"Cool," Aleks told him. If they greeted each other with anything different, the other guy would know something was really wrong. "How're things at the MC?"

"They're great. I still think you'd love it here." Vann's voice was low and rough, which added to his presence. Most of the guys who'd been locked in the cages with him had been scared of him just because of his voice alone. He sounded like a killer.

"Right. I'm so good with rules and regs."

Vann laughed. "The Army could've made you a man."

"Right. Because they did such a great job with you, asshole," Aleks muttered. "Emme's good?"

"She's great, yeah. You've got to come meet her soon."

"I will." They'd decided on a reunion six months post-Aleks's job. "Going to happen sooner than later. I met Harry's cousin today."

"You're shitting me."

"We knew he owned the building I work in. I didn't realize he looked after his own properties, or that he's friends with Inked's owners. He just got back from some overseas trip and walked into the shop today."

Both Aleks and Vann knew Brogan through pictures they'd found of him with Harry, but this update? Made even

Vann sit in silence for several moments before finally asking, "We haven't been able to figure out if Brogan's in on it—any news on that front?"

"Nothing connects Brogan to the ring. I don't think he's got any idea how Harry spends his free time and his money. But sometimes an innocent can cause more danger just by being innocent."

"Preaching to the choir, brother."

"I think I have to push him a little bit. He recognized me for sure, but he wasn't about to admit it in front of the entire tattoo parlor," Aleks continued.

"Just be careful. Anything seems weird, kill him and Harry and get the hell out of Dodge. You've got a place to cover you here anytime—president's orders."

Aleks didn't even know the Bastard Sons' president, had never met him, but the guy had literally opened his MC to Aleks should he need it. "Thanks, man. Don't worry, I'll be careful."

After they'd hung up, Aleks did a little recon online regarding Brogan but didn't find anything new or concerning. His plan was to avoid Brogan—seeing him, talking about him, obsessing over him—but after jerking off in the shower thinking about him, Aleks decided to forgo staying home.

He let his curiosity—and his anger—get the best of him and he found himself at Club X (their logo was a Saint Andrew's Cross so it fit), an upscale BDSM club. If Con's intel was correct, Brogan would definitely hang out here, not in any of the seedier clubs Aleks frequented from time to time in order to get his fix.

He'd been here once and the vibe was definitely too

"businessmen take a walk on the wild side" which screamed "inexperienced" to Aleks. He wasn't anyone's teacher. If he was going to put himself in someone's hands, he wanted them to know what the fuck they were doing.

Brogan would. Whether Aleks would turn himself over to get a firsthand view? Undecided at best.

"New in town?" the bouncer asked as Aleks approached the door.

"Not new enough," he muttered as he paid the entrance fee and was permitted through the ropes because of his looks and definitely not his charm.

Not that he gave a shit. If Brogan wasn't here, Aleks was out.

Which of course, basically ensured that Brogan *was* here, because that's how fate worked. Aleks caught sight of him as he walked toward the bar, or maybe Brogan caught sight of him first.

Aleks nodded briefly in his direction, leaned on the corner of the bar and ordered a shot and a club soda.

"Good day at work?" Brogan asked.

Aleks downed the bourbon, let it catch fire down to his belly. He waved off another shot from the bartender and switched immediately to the club soda before answering Brogan with a simple, "Yes."

Brogan nodded. "Not a big drinker?"

"Not when I'm looking to play." His voice was even. Decisive. He kept his gaze on Brogan, and Brogan smiled and turned to the bartender, who handed him a key.

Room three. Was that Brogan's special room? Aleks almost asked him but it would come out as snidely as it sounded in his own head, like he was jealous…and fuck that.

"So, let's go play." Brogan slid off his barstool and Aleks finished his club soda and nodded.

"Nothing interferes with Inked." He probably didn't need to say it, but it might piss Brogan off, which could be fun.

Brogan stared at him for a long second and then said, "Agreed. Let's go."

Right. He rolled his eyes behind Brogan's back and heard the bartender's muffled snort.

Another Dom, a big guy with a shaved head and lots of tattoos—good ones—murmured, "You get tired of him, come find me, babe."

"I will," Aleks told him, saw Brogan's shoulders stiffen.

Fun. At least it was until he was inside the room and Brogan closed and locked the door. Aleks could get out easily but it stopped people from walking in by accident.

Deep breath—not the cages, he told himself.

"Strip," Brogan told him, then stood a few feet away from him, waiting.

Aleks's heart thudded like he was a goddamned virgin, like it was his first time in a back room. It was part fear of having his entire plan blown, and for what? Curiosity? A fuck?

Why was he here with this man?

Because you still jack off thinking about the way he looked at you.

Brogan assessed him and frowned. "You're not good at following orders."

Aleks raised his chin and demanded, "Prove to me they're worth following."

Usually subs didn't demanded that a Dom prove anything to them. This just proved how right Brogan's gut had been, even all those years ago. Aleks was a couple of inches shorter than Brogan, a little broader, but in a fight? They'd be matched. In bed too, Brogan figured, because his cock had been hard from the time he'd recognized the former fighter turned tattoo artist working in the center of the place.

Brogan narrowed his eyes. "You need to be coddled? You're in the wrong place."

"Gave up my mother's tit a long time ago."

Brogan stared into Aleks's deep, dark eyes and repeated his original command. "Strip. And lie down so I can show you how much you still need. How you still crave. I've seen you perform. Now I want to see you do it at my whim."

Aleks stared back at him and began to shrug out of his clothes, leaving them draped where they fell on the floor. Brogan watched, not giving a damn about messy clothes. Order and rules weren't a part of his game. Bringing a strong man to a screaming, life-altering orgasm? Definitely. And Aleks had been at the top of his list.

Tonight was the culmination of years of fantasy. If Brogan had his way, it would only be the beginning. "Safe word."

"Orange. Where do you want me?" Aleks asked, pretending to be a well-behaved boy even through his barely contained smirk.

Brogan was going to blow Aleks's mind, whether Aleks wanted that or not. And that had nothing to do with consent. What Aleks was doing was all a mindfuck, a mental game. A fighter's weapon.

But this wasn't the ring. There was no reason for Aleks to have hands up to protect and deflect.

He pointed to the table in the middle of the room. "Lie down."

Aleks stalked to the table. God, he was beautiful. Tattoos ran along his arms, a beautiful swell of ink-covered muscle. An almost full backpiece—angel's wings that weren't overdone—completed the look…and that irony wasn't lost on Brogan.

Neither were Aleks's muscled ass and thighs. He looked powerful. Perfect. *And he knows it*, Brogan thought. "Hands over your head."

Aleks complied, stretching his arms and grabbing the center bar that came up out of the back of the table, and managed to look sleepy—even bored—although his cock was hard. "This all you got?"

Brogan couldn't resist. He leaned in, sucked the tip of Aleks's cock hard, causing him to jackknife.

"Fuck."

"Yeah, we'll get there." His voice was husky now with the taste of Aleks on his lips, salty and male and he wanted more. Giving head—without letting men come—was a skill he'd cultivated. It gave the receiver the mistaken belief that he was in control, when really he was the furthest thing from it. "Don't hold back your moans. I want to hear it all, baby."

Aleks's chest rose and fell, his struggle to regain control over his turned-traitor body obvious. Good. It was masterful to watch the struggle, but Brogan would ensure Aleks wouldn't win. That he'd love every second of losing.

"Stop moving around" was a bullshit command Brogan never understood. He wanted the man he was with moving, rutting, moaning. He wanted to see it in all its wanton glory, wanted to taste the salty pleasure and feel the impending orgasm in his own cock.

He put a palm on Aleks's chest, spread his fingers to feel the beating heart. "You want to come?"

"Yes," Aleks hissed.

"Then come," Brogan said, wrapping his palm around Aleks's cock and stroking, hard and fast.

Aleks came, exploding along his chest and Brogan's hand, thrashing around on the table…a celebration of a fight he'd both won and lost.

When he'd come down from the high of his orgasm, he stared at Brogan as he wiped his hand on one of the complimentary towels.

"Feel better?" Brogan asked.

Aleks grunted in return, but stayed in position. Waiting.

"Thanks for that. Stay as long as you need to," Brogan assured him and thought, *Here we go.*

Aleks stared at him in disbelief first and then that familiar flash of temper crossed his expression. When Brogan turned his back on the fighter, he braced for impact.

He'd wanted to pick a fight…and he'd found one.

Chapter Three

Aleks saw red. Before he could stop himself he was tackling Brogan to the ground, angry mostly at himself for allowing any show of vulnerability to his enemy.

Brogan's cousin is the enemy. Brogan? TBD.

Still, he knew who Aleks was and where he worked, which meant Harry might be tracking him as well. He had to be smart, test the man currently lying as if he was merely a content submissive underneath him. But there was nothing submissive about Brogan.

"Problem, Aleks? I'm sure the club has a complaint department."

Aleks continued to straddle him as he leaned in and asked, "Where's my cash? Or are you not in a betting mood tonight?"

At that, Brogan smiled. The bastard *smiled*. "I don't have to pay to fuck."

Bastard was going to make him spell it out. *Meanwhile, you were supposed to keep a goddamned low profile.* Christ. "You seem to like to spend your money on me." Aleks knew his words were tinged with both anger and pride, but he couldn't hide that.

Brogan's expression softened. "I didn't think you'd remember me."

"I remember a lot of things." Brogan had watched him fight in the early days. The matches at that point seemed friendly enough. Consensual, which they technically were.

Pretty fucking easy to consent when they held someone you loved and threatened to kill them unless you worked off their debt.

But Brogan hadn't known that while he'd watched Aleks, just sixteen years old. He'd just been eyeing Aleks for jerk-off material and hell, it'd obviously worked if Brogan was still this hot for him.

"There were a lot of people in the audience that night. What made you remember me?" Brogan challenged.

"Not all of them wanted to fuck me," Aleks told him. "How many nights did you jerk off thinking about me?"

"You give yourself a lot of credit." Maybe so, but Brogan's voice was husky with need when he spoke.

Aleks also felt the power coiled intensely in Brogan's body. Even if he hadn't known the man had served, he'd have been able to tell by the way Brogan had been trained to play dead at the same time he was poised to strike.

What was Aleks thinking, fucking a guy he might have to kill? If nothing else, Brogan could turn out to be collateral damage.

Or you could. "Tell me, baby—was it every night for a while there? What did you picture?"

Brogan's cock throbbed between them. Aleks was rock

hard too and the tension in the air—sexual and otherwise—was palpable as Brogan told him, "You. On your knees. My cock in your mouth. My hand twisted in your hair, holding you there, making you suck me. Fucking beautiful."

"Yeah," Aleks heard himself murmur before he leaned down to kiss Brogan and fuck, it was good. Better than he'd expected. Better than he'd wanted it to be. Especially when Brogan's hand cupped the back of his neck and held him close, deepening the kiss.

Aleks stretched out on top of Brogan, letting his weight settle, knowing Brogan could take it.

Brogan can handle you. Physically, at least.

It gave him a thrill. This kind of evenly matched fight didn't happen often and Aleks never expected it to. But when it did, like now, man, what a turn-on.

Brogan's hands traveled up and down Aleks's bare back, casually stroking, and he languidly thrust his hips up against Aleks's. The combination of Brogan's jean-covered cock rough against Aleks's bare one had him moaning in Brogan's mouth. He wasn't going to be able to handle this friction for very long before coming.

Again.

Brogan seemed to know. He stopped, rolled them so he was on top. Then he sat back on his heels and unzipped his jeans.

He leaned in again, capturing Aleks's mouth as Aleks reached down to help strip him, yanking the fabric down with hands first, then bare feet for the final push along Brogan's calves as Brogan toed off his shoes.

Then he made short work of Brogan's shirt…and that's

when the fun began. It wasn't so much about dominance. It was about who could give the most pleasure, and Aleks could come from just Brogan's kisses. They were that good, that dominating. Aleks could easily come and float away pleasantly, but his body was revved for more, for harder, and wouldn't be satisfied until he'd gotten it.

But Brogan was pulling away, yanking Aleks up onto his knees so his cock was in Aleks's direct view.

Just like Brogan's fantasy. Jesus. Aleks blew out a stuttered breath at the way Brogan was staring down at him. And then Brogan put his hand in Aleks's hair, twisting it, pushing Aleks's face forward. "Suck me. Now."

The command got Aleks harder.

Brogan watched Aleks's mouth close around his cock as Aleks stared up at him with those damned beautiful, dark eyes that held all the secrets Brogan wanted to unlock. He knew Aleks's lips would be full, bruised, swollen after taking Brogan in like this, deep-throating him, humming along the length of Brogan's cock.

"Yeah, Aleks—that's it. Take me in."

Aleks didn't break Brogan's gaze as he sucked hard along the crown of Brogan's cock before swallowing him again. Brogan loosened his grip on Aleks's hair because Aleks was doing just fine on his own, sucking Brogan's balls, licking Brogan's length before using his tongue to pump Brogan's pisshole like he was trying to stretch him open.

Brogan's legs went weak when Aleks did that. And of

course Aleks knew, smiled around his cock as he continued to drive Brogan crazy.

He wanted to come all over Aleks's chest, to rub it in, make Aleks clean everything up with his tongue. But there was time for that. Now, he needed to come, but he'd do that inside Aleks's ass.

He pulled Aleks off and tugged him up, leading him back to the table. Aleks didn't argue, got on his back as Brogan rolled the condom onto himself. Then he grabbed Aleks's hips and brought him close, put Aleks's legs over his shoulders and probed his hole.

"Yeah," Aleks hissed, his lips definitely swollen. *Debauched.* It was a damned fine look on him.

He slid inside, meeting some resistance, but Aleks shook his head, yelled, "Come on. Just fuck me. Do it." So Brogan slid in, hard, fast, and Aleks cursed and smiled. "Yeah, that's it, Brogan. Come on."

So Brogan gave him the ride of his life, wondering how Aleks could be held down so tightly, not in control at all, and yet still be so goddamned cocky.

"Come on, Brogan. Faster," Aleks demanded as he somehow managed to rut back against Brogan's cock.

"Christ, I need to tie you down so you can't move a muscle."

"Won't matter," Aleks assured him.

No, Brogan was pretty sure it wouldn't. Nothing did at this moment anyway except Aleks clenching around his cock, determined to milk Brogan to orgasm.

And Brogan was close, but Aleks was going down first. He gripped Aleks's hips more tightly, pulled him slightly off the table and slammed into him, hitting his gland over and over until Aleks's eyes rolled back in his head and he shot, all over his chest. Brogan paused for a second, leaned forward to lick Aleks's come and then kiss him, letting Aleks taste himself.

"Dirty," Aleks murmured. "I like it."

So did Brogan. And it only took a couple more thrusts before he was coming, muttering Aleks's name as he did so.

Aleks was stunned. Lips swollen and sore (worth it), ass equally so for the latter (worth it) but cuddling with the man whose cousin he planned on killing?

Worth it.

Dammit.

Separate the two. Take your pleasure. The cousin deserved the pain. "You're not like any Dom I've known."

"You're not exactly sub material," Brogan pointed out, sounding half drunk, and Aleks felt like he sounded, drowsy and content and still wanting to do it all over again.

They were tangled on the ground. Bruised. And Aleks still told himself he could use this...somehow. Especially if he could get more sex. More of this feeling.

He'd had sex regularly for eight years since the fights ended, but the feeling? That had been the missing component. Why hadn't he realized that until just now?

Because your body feels rested for the first time. Your mind too.

He pushed himself up onto his elbows and Brogan raised his brows. "I've got to go. Early day tomorrow," Aleks told him.

Brogan shifted and got up off the floor easily, putting a hand down to help Aleks too.

Aleks ignored it, because he'd shown too much weakness for one night.

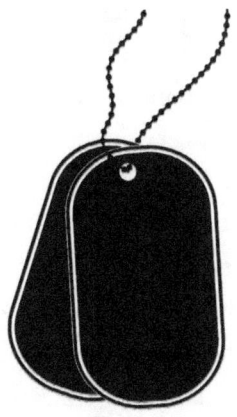

Chapter Four

Brogan strolled into Inked the following afternoon. It was empty at the moment, save for two employees, but Brogan knew the real money in this place wasn't about midday afternoon walk-ins—it was in its night and weekend crowds.

"Can I help you?" Becca, the pretty blonde piercer with the delicate flowered sleeve, asked with a smile. "We've got appointments open for this afternoon."

From the corner, Aleks laughed. "This isn't his *thing*," he told Becca, making her smile.

"Is he *your* thing, Aleks?" she shot back.

"Touché," Brogan murmured and she said, "Take your time—I'll be in the back, cleaning up."

Aleks rolled his eyes and walked over to the front desk as she ambled away, glancing over her shoulder a couple of times before disappearing. "Like she thinks we're going to fuck right here."

"I'd be all right with that."

Aleks's cheeks darkened. So did his eyes. "Forget something last night?"

"No. I'd planned on coming here and asking you out to dinner. Tonight."

"Way to give notice."

"I would've asked before you left, but you took off pretty fast. Do you have plans tonight?"

"I don't get it. People usually go to X looking for a fuck, not a dinner date," Aleks said roughly.

"Is that the only reason you tracked me down?" Brogan asked, unaffected by Aleks's words or tone, and hell, did anything throw the fucker?

"You've got some ego there."

"You're not saying I'm wrong." Brogan leaned across the counter. "Dinner? Tonight—eight o'clock. Mario's. Reservation's under my name."

And then he pushed away and left before Aleks could say anything like *No* or *Go fuck yourself* or *See you tonight*.

Brogan had a regular table at Mario's, toward the back of the place in a private corner. He didn't take clients here, just friends, sometimes lovers, but there hadn't been many of those he'd wanted to spend time with outside the bedroom.

The fact that Aleks had remembered him? Brogan could only think of this as meant to be. In his world there were no coincidences, and whatever seemed like one couldn't be ignored. In the military, it could mean the difference between life or death in the field. In business, it was winning or losing a deal.

In life? It could mean finding the guy you'd been thinking

about every time you jerked off in the shower.

"I'll have a beer—Stella," he told the server.

"Same." Aleks voice was deep. Dark and dangerous, just like the man himself. He nodded at the waiter and then took a seat across from Brogan.

They'd spent more time fucking than talking, and Brogan didn't know if Aleks would be uncomfortable when they saw each other. Because dinner was usually the prelude for sex. In Brogan's world, it rarely worked that way.

Stopping by the tattoo shop instead of calling assured Brogan that he'd gotten under Aleks's skin enough that he'd be here, if nothing else, to tell Brogan off. And that would be hot too.

"I can see why you're a regular here." Aleks put the cloth napkin on his lap, looking quite at home.

And Brogan definitely needed to find out more. Although Mario's wasn't upscale, it was more formal than most and Brogan tended to forget that, until the men he brought here seemed uncomfortable with the variety of flatware, the formality of the waiters and the like.

Not Aleks. He looked as if he could've been born into this.

"It's a great place," Brogan agreed. "Long day at work?"

"So we're going with small talk?" Aleks asked in what Brogan had come to know in a short time as his typically blunt way. "Yeah, a full day. Back-to-back appointments from nine this morning until about an hour ago."

Aleks's hair was still damp from a recent shower. He wore black leather pants that looked more rocker than fashion, but Brogan bet he got a lot of looks walking in. He planned on appreciating the pants more when they were lying on his floor. "Who taught you?"

"Mostly self-taught. Then I took on an apprenticeship. I had a knack for it."

"I'd say so." Just then, the waiter brought out an array of different dishes. "I hope you don't mind—I usually just trust the chef to send me out a variety of his best."

Aleks nodded. "Definitely a regular. And this works for me."

There was a comfortable semi-silence broken with more small talk about food as they indulged in the pasta and meat dishes, with good, crusty bread dipped in oil. As they ate, David, the chef, came to the table, and Brogan suspected it was because he wanted to meet Aleks.

Not that he could blame him. "David, this is Aleks. Aleks, this is the owner and chef."

Aleks shook David's hand. "Your place is great and the food's phenomenal."

David beamed. "You've got good taste." He glanced over at Brogan and winked. "In food, at least."

Aleks laughed, and damn, it was a nice sound. Brogan rolled his eyes at David. "Thanks for everything."

"Come back any time," David told Aleks. To Brogan, he added, "I'm sure I'll see you here tomorrow."

"No doubt," Brogan answered, then admitted to Aleks once they were alone, "I'm a disaster in the kitchen beyond the basics, but I love good food."

Aleks sat back as the plates were collected. When the waiter left them, he said, "I'm a pretty good cook. Not this level but I learned to fend for myself in the kitchen pretty early on."

"Were your parents working?"

Aleks shook his head. "My mom wasn't a good cook."

"Any brothers or sisters?"

Aleks looked into the distance, somewhere over Brogan's shoulder when he said, "I had a younger brother. He's dead."

And then he looked right into Brogan's eyes and he felt a shot of Aleks's raw pain run through him. Whatever happened, whenever it happened, Aleks wasn't over it. Would never be, judging by that reaction. "I'm sorry."

"Yeah, me too." He set down his empty beer bottle. "I don't want to talk about this anymore."

"I get it."

Aleks's eyes bore into his. "You lost someone too?"

"My parents. I was fifteen."

"Shit. Sorry."

"Yeah, me too," he echoed Aleks's sentiment. "They were good people. It was an accident—rainy night. My dad probably had a glass of wine too many and it was a perfect storm. That's when I moved in with my cousin and his family. Or that's when they sent me away to the same boarding school Harry was in."

At the mention of Harry's name, Aleks went still, but then he said, "Harry's parents didn't like kids?"

"Not at all. We were heirs. But hey, I survived. Went into the military instead of business school, but they couldn't say much about it. I inherited my fortune at eighteen and from there it was up to me."

"But you're part of the family business."

The Montgomery-Johnstone name was very well known, so it wasn't a surprise that Aleks knew about his wealth, his family or the business. He didn't seem impressed by it, but rather, simply making conversation. "To an extent. I branched out into other areas I was more interested in. I'm not a nine-to-five office guy. That's more Harry's gig."

"Right." Aleks stared at him. "I don't want to talk anymore."

"About Harry?"

"About anything." He stood, paid the check in cash, leaving a generous amount for a tip. It was, Brogan figured, his way of demonstrating to Brogan that he didn't appreciate being summoned to dinner. That he wouldn't be bought.

Brogan definitely appreciated the sentiment. "How about a drink at my place?"

Aleks narrowed his eyes. "Is that code for sex?"

"Definitely."

Aleks nodded. "I took a cab."

"Me too. I'm not too far." They began to walk, an easy silence as they enjoyed the early spring weather. Brogan's place was about six long blocks from the restaurant, and they passed several bars along the way. It was a Thursday night, so there were a lot of people stumbling around, having enjoyed happy hour and extending it well into the evening.

A few guys began following them. Brogan made them instantly as being trouble and not just guys walking home. Aleks had gotten the same feeling but they kept their stride the same, not letting on that they knew what was coming. Silently, they made their plan with a glance and a hand motion Brogan recognized instantly.

Stand down.

Why Aleks knew military terminology surprised him fleetingly, but he was more focused on the fact that he was now supposed to stand there and watch Aleks take on three guys? But he wasn't going to argue. He'd be here in case Aleks decided he needed backup.

Turned out, he didn't. As Brogan watched, Aleks stopped two of the men in their tracks as they went to grab both him and Aleks. The third guy took off running when he saw Aleks in action.

Brogan had the opposite reaction, wanted to get as close as possible to Aleks.

"Don't fucking take shit that doesn't belong to you," Aleks told one of them, right in his ear as he held onto the guy's throat in a viselike grip. The other was on the ground, under Aleks's boot. "Got it? You need money, you work for it. Because you've just run into the wrong motherfucker to rob."

The guy looked ready to piss himself, probably had a little already. Brogan stood watch in case either of them pulled a weapon. They were maybe twenty, and could be doing this more for sport than out of need. But they'd been drinking, and hopefully this made them learn their lesson.

Aleks released both men and they scampered away, the poor guy on the ground crawl-walking as fast as he could.

"I guess I was the damsel in distress," Brogan said as they began walking again, Aleks appearing unscathed by the incident, save for the anger radiating off him.

"You need to be coddled tonight?" Aleks asked finally, the usual smirk on his face as they walked through the underground garage as an easy cut-through to the elevator.

The security guard nodded at Brogan, took note of Aleks surreptitiously, no doubt so he could easily recall him again for security purposes. Brogan liked the security but didn't like his guests being harassed—he'd made that clear.

Once in the private elevator, Brogan tugged Aleks against him. "You need to work off more of that steam?"

"Definitely."

At least he was honest.

How about a drink at my place?

When Brogan had invited him home at the restaurant, Aleks told himself that he could think of it as work. Recon.

With your dick.

Still, his uncertainty about agreeing to Brogan's invitation, coupled with the threat of being followed, had Aleks on edge. But he'd decided a long time ago that he'd no longer fight— he would simply put a stop to whoever tried to fight him, quickly and decisively.

He was all kinds of ramped-up adrenaline and need, and by the time they arrived at Brogan's he was ready to get naked in the elevator. Obviously Brogan was ready for he same since he pushed Aleks against the back of the elevator and yanked his shirt off before kissing him. As Brogan's mouth took his, Brogan's hands were opening Aleks's pants and he was more than glad he hadn't bothered with underwear.

It was a few minutes before either of them acknowledged that the elevator door had opened and they did so reluctantly, Brogan groaning before letting go of him.

Aleks took a deep breath and followed him. He knew Brogan had money and it wasn't on display but a private elevator to a penthouse in the sky didn't come cheap.

Did my blood—Brad's blood—pay for this? Aleks shuddered at the thought, the betrayal, and suddenly felt too fucking naked.

Brogan touched his shoulder. "Hey, are you okay?"

Keep it together, he ordered himself. "Just a chill."

"I'll fix that," Brogan promised.

Aleks wished that could be true but realized that a part of his brain—the part that wasn't inside his cock—had walked into Brogan's place prepared for a trap. An ambush. Even if it didn't happen tonight, this could be a sizing up.

Maybe Harry had grown suspicious after Vann took out the fight's support staff, and they were looking to off the fighters who could ID them.

A long shot, but Aleks's life was built on them. If Brogan had been in on it…

But the hanging between life and death with every orgasm? *Infuckingtoxicating.*

If Brogan was playing a game, Aleks could play along. "Do you own this building?"

Brogan gave a short laugh. "Not yet. I like to keep personal and business separate. It's easier that way."

"What about that big building downtown with your name on it? I'd imagine they'd let you walk through the halls naked," Aleks said.

"Probably, but I work from home. In there." Brogan pointed to a half-closed door. "I mean, yeah, I have office space in the other building but that's for support staff. I rarely go in there unless I have a meeting about my family's stuff."

"So you mainly do real estate."

"For investment, yes. I started off buying buildings when

I came out of the military and found I really enjoyed it. It's competitive. There's always a surprise."

"Aren't the tenants a pain in the ass though?" Aleks asked.

"Your bosses are pretty nice."

"And they pay."

"The ones who don't are outed pretty quickly."

Aleks nodded. "Bet they are."

Brogan wanted to ask what Aleks meant by that, but with Aleks more information typically came from continuing the conversation rather than demanding explanation. But Aleks didn't give him a chance to continue anything before saying, "Look, I've got an early day tomorrow."

Brogan thought about forcing the issue, about shoving Aleks against the wall and holding his hands over his head and fucking him, hard and fast. Aleks would probably allow himself to be convinced, but there was something in his eyes, something dangerous that let Brogan know it wasn't the best idea.

So he nodded instead and pulled out his phone. "Your number?"

Aleks hesitated briefly before giving it. Brogan called it immediately and it rang in Aleks's pocket. "You didn't trust me?" Aleks asked.

Brogan smiled. "Give me a reason to."

Chapter Five

When Aleks walked into Inked the next morning, it was more than obvious Becca had filled everyone in on Brogan's visit and dinner invitation. Because Con was there purely for the show, waiting on one of the couches and calling out to Aleks, "Are you fucking our landlord?"

"Jesus Christ, Con!" Quinn roared, Becca and James, the other tattoo artist, laughed, and Aleks was just grateful the shop wasn't open to customers yet.

"What?" Con shrugged at Quinn in feigned innocence. "It's a simple question." He turned back to Aleks. "You know we pay rent, right? He doesn't have to take it out of your ass."

"God, you're an idiot. I'm marrying an idiot," Quinn groaned.

Con laughed and didn't dispute the idiot comment.

"They're not just fucking. They're dating," Becca chimed in.

"Difference?" Con asked.

"They go to nice dinner places."

Con nodded. "The guy's got bank."

Yes, and so did Aleks. He just buried his trust fund better than most.

"I'm betting they have another date this week," Becca said to everyone in the shop except Aleks, who now leaned against the counter, content to sit back and watch everyone discuss his sex life while he finished his coffee.

Inked was taking under/over bets on Aleks and Brogan by the time he'd left work that evening. It'd been a long day, with no Brogan visits or calls, which had Becca more upset than Aleks.

He needed to get his shit together, put himself back on track and figure out his next steps. Brogan's place hadn't yielded any real surprises, and it was still Aleks's gut instinct that Brogan wasn't involved in the underground fighting.

Illegal underground fight clubs were everywhere. Most of them boasted consensual players who fought each other for money and underground fame. Maybe one percent of all the fight clubs were deathmatches, which made them hard to trace.

It helped the owners of these places that most of the fighters ended up dead, leaving no witnesses who'd be willing to talk to the police. But Aleks made inroads at enough local boxing gyms to get the inside track…mainly because they all wanted to recruit him to fight underground.

Tonight, he went into one of those gyms. It was in one of the more run-down sections of the city which made it a draw to those types of fights. He had a membership and worked out there at least once a week in order to keep current.

Tonight, he hit the jackpot. Exactly what he'd suspected. Even though Vann had killed Harry's men, there were enough shitty-assed people in the world to populate another one of Harry's venues.

"Special Edition," one of the men told him in passing. "Do you know anyone?"

"I can get you some names," Aleks said.

"Don't take too long. Spots filling up fast."

Yeah, I'll bet. Aleks finished his workout, feeling sick to his stomach. Special Edition was code for "young fighters." Under eighteen.

Aleks had been recruited for a Special Edition ring. And recruitment was very different from anything any of those boys had ever experienced.

This meant that Harry was due back soon—because he brought his important clients to these fights. He was gearing up for a brand-new shiny edition of the deathmatches.

Aleks would kill him before recruitment got underway.

After a long, hot shower, Aleks called Vann.

"How's Harry's cousin?" was the first thing his friend asked after their usual greeting.

"Didn't see him today." It wasn't until Aleks said that out loud that he realized he was annoyed at that fact. *Dammit.*

"Do you need to cuddle?"

"Fuck off," Aleks muttered and Vann laughed. "Everyone at work is taking bets on me and Brogan. We went to dinner last night."

"Dinner?"

Aleks sighed inwardly and admitted, "I went to his place afterward. You know—for recon."

With your dick...

Vann paused for a long moment—his friend would never judge him, but would protect him to the death.

Finally, Vann told him, "You're playing with fire, Aleks," and his use of the word *fire* was purposeful. They'd both lost everything in those flames—except each other.

"It's the only way I know how." He paused. "There's another match I got invited to." He explained what he'd learned at the gym. "I wish we had more leads. I just don't get how none of the men admitted to starting the fire."

"Yeah, you'd think they'd admit their sins on their deathbeds—or at least try to use a confession to get out of dying. Doesn't mean they weren't lying sacks of shit though," Vann reasoned. "Do you need my help?"

"What, you think I can't handle it?"

"I know you can. Question is, should you have to? Because it sounds like you like this Brogan guy and none of this is great for family relations."

"Doesn't matter. It's not like it's serious."

"So you're just using this guy?"

He ground out, "Yes," and Vann gave a short laugh before telling him, "Right. Keep saying that until you believe it."

Then he hung up before Aleks could toss off a retort. He sacked out on the couch and watched mindless TV so his subconscious could be free to formulate a plan or pick up on a sign from the universe.

Anything, at this point—because he knew what he needed to do, and he had a time frame…and a giant complication in the form of a blond-haired, blue-eyed man.

Aleks had compartmentalized his life into thirds for a long time. Since the cages, it had been about past and present. The third and final missing piece—future—hadn't mattered because he refused to look that far ahead. Until he did what he needed to do, he would be stuck in the past, barely noticing the present.

And that was o-fucking-kay with him.

And he'd keep telling himself that until he believed it.

He'd do so, because all he had were memories, not pictures, of his brother, Berdy. When he'd gone back to the apartment they'd lived in, post-fighting, it had been rented to other people and no one had any knowledge of where his and Berdy's things had gone. Aleks knew they'd been effectively sanitized—and Vann's things had met the same fate.

Berdy was born blind. Aleks remembered their father not exactly treating Berdy badly, but pretty well ignoring him, knowing that Berdy could never follow into the lifestyle of a Russian mobster.

Of course, Berdy would've been a better choice than Aleks—given time, Berdy's talent for tactics would've shown through. His brother could see better than any sighted person Aleks had ever known. That gave Aleks less comfort than anything when he thought about Berdy's death…being locked away, without any stimulation but what he could hear. Berdy wasn't helpless, but he was at a disadvantage in certain situations.

Aleks always hoped that because Berdy couldn't identify

anyone, he might be let go. But fate had other plans.

Aleks was a "poor little rich kid." At least that's how he'd been referred to on the streets. He was the son of a mafia boss who'd been killed in the line of duty for the mob. When their mama moved them out of the nest of mob neighborhoods and into a new area of Coney Island, she'd really thought things would be better. She did so to hide the fact that she had millions in offshore bank accounts. She'd wanted to get away from mob activity and instead, Aleks found himself in the center of it.

After Dad died, Berdy would stay home with Mom, paving the way for Aleks's early life of a little bit of crime and a lot of sex.

He'd known he was gay from the second he understood just what 'gay' meant. He'd been fourteen, fifteen, sixteen, hitting bars and gay clubs, illegal underground ones full of underage sex, money and drugs. It was all about the sex for him, but money too, because his family needed it—because his mom refused to touch those offshore millions for fear of triggering too much attention to their family. Aleks figured out from a young age that combining work and play made for an easier job.

The most important club was the underground speakeasy-type on the corner. There, he could run messages between two of the upper echelon soldiers of the crime lord Aleks's father had answered to.

Aleks didn't want to be on that same path, but the money was good, the prestige important to keep his mother and Berdy from being hurt. He'd always been bigger for his age, and especially in the gay underground, youth was prized.

He was always willing.

But then the men who ran the fight club had taken Berdy, and Aleks had gone to the address he'd been given and turned himself over willingly for a two-year sentence to save him.

Now, Aleks closed his eyes and thought about Brogan, the fights, the cage—because they were all inexorably entwined.

Brogan had a lankier in build back then, with shorter, dirty blond hair and blue-as-fuck eyes that Aleks had been sure he'd remember till the day he died. In that cage, he'd thought about Brogan through long nights when he couldn't sleep, when the guys around him were crying or screaming because they'd gone insane.

He and Vann vowed early on to help each other, probably because they recognized their inner strength. Aleks knew better than to try to save the other twenty or so guys there—most of them wouldn't make it. And from there, it would be a never-ending, revolving door of new guys.

The guys who made it through were trying to intimidate Aleks, to break him down so they'd win the deathmatches. They were all competing for life, theirs and a loved one's. They all had the strongest motivation possible, but Vann always reminded him that they had the strongest minds.

He and Vann had different backgrounds but the story was similar—young boys in a poor neighborhood, surrounded by Russian mafia activity.

Aleks's brother, younger by two years, had been taken to ensure Aleks's cooperation. Vann's first love, Lola, had been taken as well, and they'd been killed that same night Vann pulled Aleks out of the fire.

"Do you think Berdy and Lola became friends?" he'd asked

Vann once.

"There's no way they wouldn't have," Vann told him immediately, and even if he'd been lying, Aleks was forever grateful for the answer.

Chapter Six

Aleks was pacing his apartment the following night. He'd gone to work, listened to everyone yammer on about him and Brogan, and he'd gone to the gym, where he hadn't been able to get out enough of his frustration.

He was dreaming about the guy, for chrissakes—hot, torturous dreams that had him waking up hard as fuck and unsatisfied. He thought about going to X, taking another Dom—any Dom—up on their offer. Or maybe Brogan would be there...

Or maybe Brogan's waiting for you to call him.

"Cold day in hell," he muttered. And then he picked up his cell and dialed. When Brogan answered, Aleks just said, "Hey."

"I thought you lost my number," Brogan said.

"Phone works both ways," Aleks told him.

"Want to come over?" Brogan asked without missing a beat.

No way. "Yeah."

"Have you eaten?"

"Not yet."

"I'll order some takeout. Chinese okay?"

"That's fine," Aleks bit out.

"See you in a few," Brogan said.

After he hung up, Aleks stared at the cell phone in his hand as though it was the traitor who'd dialed Brogan all by itself. Then he tossed it on the table, showered and went to Brogan's.

He didn't realize that he was stalking into Brogan's apartment, angry as fuck. He'd gotten more worked up on the way over, and all he wanted to do was forget. And that made him feel guilty because he shouldn't want to forget any of it.

"Hey." Brogan tilted his head. "You seem…"

"Frustrated," Aleks answered before he could stop himself.

"I can help with that."

Aleks snorted. "Right."

Brogan moved closer to him, so close that he was able to lean into Aleks's cheek. "Right."

Brogan could tell from the phone call that Aleks was wound tight, but it was painfully apparent from the way he'd stalked into the apartment. Somehow, Brogan needed to turn Aleks into the prey.

That's what Aleks wanted anyway. So Brogan nipped his earlobe, then licked along Aleks's neck. Aleks moved involuntarily closer to him, looking for full-body contact and Brogan gave it to him, put a hand on Aleks's ass to keep him close while murmuring, "I want to put you over my knee and spank the frustration right out of you," against Aleks's cheek.

He felt Aleks shudder against him and he'd hit on something. Whether Aleks answered with words or not, he'd given himself—his *wants*—away.

"You want it—come on. Let me help."

Aleks found his voice, said, "No" loudly as he pulled back and shook his head hard, like he was trying to deny his need to himself as much as he was to Brogan.

Brogan let Aleks keep some distance between them. "I can wait all night. But that?" He motioned between Aleks's legs. "Probably having a tough time."

"I have self-control."

"Right." Brogan looked him up and down, then went to sit in the nearest comfortable chair and patted his thighs. "Come on, baby. Just give it up to me. No harm, no foul. I promise you'll thank me. I know I'll be thanking you for a hell of a show."

Aleks's cheeks were flushed, with desire and fear and that ache of need Brogan knew so well in the pit of his belly. Finally, Aleks took a step forward. Something changed, the set of his shoulders, maybe, showed a determination, an anger…a willingness. Only Aleks could combine all three so well and still appear as in control as he was not.

Still, Brogan pushed. "Move slower. I'm upping the amount of smacks you get every time you make me wait."

Aleks's cheeks flushed. "Please…"

Right. Please *yes*.

Please don't make me do this was really *please force me into this*. Brogan had been playing the Dom/sub game long enough to tell the difference. "Is that your new safe word?"

"No. Same," Aleks managed. "Orange."

"Good. Come on, then."

Aleks swallowed with a visible pull, then took his shirt off and tossed it aside. He bent down and untied his boots, sliding out of them easily. Barefoot, in jeans only, hair tousled and face angry and hopeful, and Brogan knew Aleks was the best-looking man he'd ever seen.

Finally, Aleks unzipped his jeans and pulled them down enough to expose himself. Only then did he say, "I can't. Not like that."

He pointed to the floor, the couch, the bed. Brogan wondered if he should let Aleks call that shot and decided positioning wasn't as important as giving Aleks a safe release for his pent-up anger. "Fine. The bed. Everything off, though. And get on all fours."

Aleks complied fairly quickly, but there was just enough purposeful hesitation to ensure he'd get punished for noncompliance. When Brogan walked into his bedroom, the sight of Aleks on all fours, on his bed, ass facing him, was perfect.

He went into the bathroom, put lube in his pocket and brought a towel over to the bed. He put it under Aleks, then ran his hand down Aleks's bare back, let it travel slowly down to his ass, where it rested on his left ass cheek.

Aleks shuddered again. His head was up and he was looking straight ahead when Brogan brought his hand down firmly on his ass, an open-palmed swat that made Aleks groan and his skin redden. The second smack had him hanging his head down. By the fifth, he was breathing hard, swaying a little.

Brogan reached into his pocket for the lube, snapped the lid open with a flick of his thumb and squirted it on his fingers. He threw the tube down and slid two generously lubed digits inside Aleks, causing him to rut against the invasion. "Good. Fuck my fingers. I'll add another if you're good."

Aleks did as he asked and was rewarded with a third to open him and brush his prostate. And when Aleks began rocking his hips and getting lost in the rhythm, Brogan pulled out and brought his other hand down on Aleks's ass, over and over again, until Aleks was squirming and yelling and cursing...and moaning in pure goddamned pleasure. "Brogan, please... I...need. I fucking...need."

"Don't come," Brogan told him firmly, knowing there was no way Aleks could hold back. "Don't you dare."

But it only took two more smacks before Aleks's orgasm hit him. His body tensed and he cursed again, and he came, all over himself mostly. His arms and legs trembled visibly and the tension finally left his body, leaving him a limp, wobbly mess.

Exactly the way Brogan wanted him. "Want to fuck you," he warned.

"Good," Aleks muttered, his head still down.

"On your back." He rolled a condom on as Aleks complied, and Brogan pulled him down to the edge of the bed, put Aleks's legs on his shoulders so his cock lined up perfectly with Aleks's hole. He pushed his cock inside Aleks's already slick channel and Aleks's body arched upward, accepting the invasion and welcoming it with a soft, satisfied groan.

Brogan grabbed Aleks's hips to hold him in place as he pistoned his own hips, giving Aleks no escape from the constant pressure on his gland. It was no doubt sensitive as hell, and he watched as Aleks's expression told the story of skating the thin line between pain and pleasure.

Pleasure won out. Or hell, maybe the pain did it, but Aleks came before Brogan. It was mainly a dry orgasm, but getting to watch his body spasm was what pushed Brogan over the edge. He pulled out, ripped the condom off and came with an aching climax all over Aleks's chest and belly, his gaze never leaving Aleks's face.

Aleks never looked away either. And when Brogan could fucking breathe again, he let his gaze wander to Aleks's chest, his own come mixed with Brogan's, and Brogan couldn't help but rub them together and into Aleks's skin where he already had a tattoo made up of interlocking rings, marking him further.

After a shower, where Aleks mainly just stood under the hot water to let Brogan prop him up and wash him, the food arrived.

He was finally, momentarily, satiated. And starving. He wore only a soft pair of borrowed sweats, and with Brogan dressed the same, they sat next to each other on the couch in Brogan's living room with the food spread on the coffee table. They ate right out of the containers, with chopsticks, passing the noodles and chicken and beef back and forth.

"Good stuff. From Tasty Kitchen?"

Brogan nodded. "The best takeout in the city."

"Agreed."

Brogan had Yuengling beer too, which Aleks always appreciated. His ass stung a little, but in that good, hot way that reminded him that he'd gotten what he'd come for.

He felt more focused than he had before. He'd played. Now it was time for work. When he'd eaten enough, he stood, stretched and began to survey the apartment again the way he hadn't had the opportunity to the other night. Brogan sat back on the couch, not seeming to mind Aleks walking around to check out at the family photos, looking closely at the pictures of people who appeared to be Brogan's parts. Military ones. None of Harry or Harry's family.

Now, he picked up one of the framed photos to get a closer look at Brogan, wearing his camouflage war paint, a grim expression, his rifle by his side. He was surrounded by several men, all dressed exactly the same. But Aleks could pick Brogan out of a crowd just by his eyes—so blue they glowed in the picture.

"That was in South America," Brogan said finally.

Aleks stared at it a few more seconds before putting it down and walking back to the couch. "I'm guessing you can't get more specific than that."

Brogan shook his head no. "Good guys in my unit. We stayed together for four years."

Aleks had heard a similar sentiment from Vann, but Vann had both enlisted—and left—for a very specific purpose. Why a man with Brogan's money and connections would? Aleks needed to find out.

"Why'd you sign up in the first place? Legacy?" Aleks asked him.

Brogan hadn't been sure that Aleks wouldn't bolt post-shower, or even post-dinner, but he seemed content to pad around the apartment. Prowling, really...and asking questions. Far more than he'd asked during their date. "No. I'm the first in my family to serve. They weren't very happy when I enlisted."

He could still clearly remember the disapproval he'd faced when he'd told his aunt and uncle he was seriously considering the Army instead of college. There was, of course, the pressure from his uncle and Harry to go to the 'right' college, the 'right' frat, to make the connections that would help him dive right into the cutthroat big business world post-graduation. But he'd wanted *out*—wanted to see the world but not in the way Harry was planning on. No, Brogan wanted to get his hands dirty. Wanted to pull his weight. Wanted to forget he was a rich kid from a rich family and prove himself, rebuild from the ground up.

The military had been helpful in that regard, and more than a little humbling.

"Special Forces just seems...unnecessary," his uncle had said in his early attempts to be diplomatic. "Military service is honorable. But the company needs you back, not wallowing around playing soldier."

Brogan had wanted to bite out, "I'm not playing," but he'd done what he'd learned in the military: smiled and nodded... and then did what he wanted to at the first opportunity that it wouldn't harm himself or anyone else.

And then he'd gone into Rangers training.

"That must've been tough, not having their approval." Aleks looked at him with an expression Brogan couldn't quite place, but he swore there was some approval of his own in there.

"I came to the realization that I couldn't live the life someone else wanted for me, family business or not. I had to figure out who I was, what I wanted. And trust me, college and the family business would've been the easy road. Ranger training was no walk in the park." None of it had been, but he wouldn't trade a second of it.

"I've got a good friend who served. Said it was exactly what he'd needed." Aleks's eyes were somewhere far away for a brief second. "So why did you get out?"

Brogan took a breath and decided to be completely honest. "Because Harry was mismanaging the charities my parents worked so hard to put into place. I couldn't be all over the world, unable to gain access to the company. I learned what I needed to in the military. I gave to it and it gave me exactly what I needed. I took those lessons and I apply them daily to the world around me and my business," Brogan said.

"Would've been easier to stay in, yes?" Aleks said finally.

"Much," Brogan admitted hollowly. "But I've always been a realist at heart."

Brogan believed in what he'd said about the military—he'd spoken the words from a place of fierce pride and independence, and Aleks could see the struggle he'd faced.

It was interesting, and important to Aleks to know that

Brogan had evidence that his cousin wasn't an honorable man. Still, it was a far cry from believing Harry mismanaged charitable funds to being told that he owned and operated a fighting ring that kidnapped and killed. "So you came back and fixed the charities. But you're doing real estate too."

"Right. I manage the charities and oversee the businesses with Harry, although he's more day to day on that front along with my uncle. It leaves me time for real estate. I fell into it with an impulse buy and realized I enjoyed it."

"Obviously you're good at it."

Brogan nodded. "I've got a knack—and I like the thrill of the deal."

"You like control," Aleks muttered and Brogan laughed.

"I can't argue with you. But yes, there's something about owning a place, knowing it's yours, that you can't beat. Because then you have control over it—your own home." Brogan paused. "You're renting, right?"

Aleks rolled his eyes. "Right."

"You should buy your place. Buy a place."

"Thanks, Dad, but—"

Brogan was on him, pushing his back into the couch cushions and lying half on him. "Funny—it seemed like you were looking for a daddy."

Brogan said it wryly but Aleks couldn't argue that he'd hit the damned nail on the head. He liked Brogan's strength. It soothed him. He could relax into the sex, knowing he wasn't going to accidentally break Brogan.

But Aleks was getting too comfortable with Brogan.

You don't have to tell him you killed Harry. He doesn't ever have to know.

Right. Keeping that big of a secret from someone you lo—

Fuck. He'd just freaked himself the fuck out. On several levels.

Chapter Seven

Weeks passed. Aleks fell into a semi-regular routine of seeing Brogan a couple of times a week—usually after telling himself that he was going to end it before it got any further.

But it kept moving, like a goddamned shark.

Now, Brogan was on a business trip for a week, so Aleks had time to collect his thoughts undistracted. He would use it wisely.

He'd had met a lot of characters along the way to becoming a sought-after tattoo artist. Although he had to stay under the radar and give up some more public opportunities, for obvious reasons, it also gave him access to some of the more "creative" types.

And when he met these various creative types, be they computer thieves, pickpockets, mafia drones and the like, Aleks made sure he learned from them. If nothing else, he made sure to trade favors so he could call on one of them if needed.

Right now, he'd have to rely on what he'd learned about hacking. Calling someone in to check out Harry's bank account transfers would mean there was someone else Aleks would have to watch out for.

First, he bounced the IP address all across the globe. Impossible to trace, even with Harry's massive resources.

He connected with Harry's cell phone and computer, plus GPS. Somewhere, he'd find a list of names of boys who would soon find family members or loved ones kidnapped.

He also found what he'd been hoping to—a trail created to make it look as though Brogan was hiding something in a shell company. It was the only property linked to anything suspicious, and Aleks wondered if Harry was covering his tracks and making it look as though Brogan was investing in the illegal fighting ring?

It made sense. If Brogan caught on to Harry's illegal fighting ring activities, Harry would blackmail him into not going to the police. Brogan would be indicting both of them.

"Dammit." Aleks sat back, his head ready to explode. He was late to work, so he closed down the computer and walked there to try to clear his head.

It only made things worse. He needed someone on the inside for this…and it couldn't be him. Couldn't be Vann. Who the fuck did he know who was crazy enough to go undercover and work for a psycho…

Con called, "Morning, sunshine," when Aleks walked into Inked.

"Right. A psycho for a psycho," Aleks muttered.

Con frowned. "You're looking crazy. Which means you're up to something no good. And I want in."

"I could use your help," Aleks admitted, thankful they were the only two in the shop at the moment.

Con pointed at him. "I told Quinn you were dangerous."

Aleks didn't bother disputing that truth. Con was equally as dangerous, maybe on a whole other level, even. "I'd never ask. But it's not for profit."

Con nodded. "Cancel your morning. When Becca gets here, let's head to the diner to talk. I never know what the hell Quinn wires to try to keep me out of trouble."

Half an hour later, Con's eyes were murderous as Aleks laid out the story. It was the first time he'd ever told it, and he could feel Con's anger. He was surprised everyone within fifty feet wasn't running from the palpable rage.

"Tell me what you need me to do and how to pull it off," Con finally said through gritted teeth.

"If something happened to you—"

"I can't live with myself knowing this shit. You can't either."

"Quinn?"

"I'll tell him. Afterward," Con added. "You wouldn't have come to me if you didn't think I could do it."

Aleks stared at him. "A friend of mine will want to run a check on you. Will he find anything?"

"Just my impeccable service record." Con sat back. "Look, I'm running black ops. Quinn knows a little bit. I'm just doing enough to stay in practice so I don't go goddamned nuts. But I've been buried by the best of them. I can get whatever cover you need me to."

Relief coursed though Aleks. "I was supposed to do this alone but—"

Con leaned forward. "You have friends, Aleks. All you needed to do was ask."

Vann had told him the same thing. "Thanks."

"What about Brogan?"

"What about him?"

Con rolled his eyes. "Aleks, come on. If he's not involved, fuck, you've got to tell him what's happening with his cousin. The Brogan that Quinn and I know is a damned good guy. I'm not saying that appearances can't be deceiving, but at some point, if things continue with him the way they've been, you're going to have to tell him about Harry. About you. I'm not seeing a way around that."

Neither does Vann. Aleks laughed harshly. "Yeah, I'll fill him in on all of this over dinner when he comes back from his trip. Maybe we'll catch a movie afterward. Christ, I really fucked up."

"You're falling for him. That fucks everyone up," Con reasoned quietly, saying out loud what Aleks had been refusing to admit to himself for the past month.

And even though Aleks wanted to tell Con to go screw himself, that he didn't know what he was talking about, that Aleks wouldn't fall in love that easily, never mind with someone from Harry's family, he couldn't. Instead, he managed, "Vann did his job."

"Yes, and you'll do yours. You couldn't control the circumstances." Con glanced around. "You don't know that you haven't been traced the whole time."

Aleks couldn't even ask why him and not Vann. He knew why—he was the rich one, the one with the old-school Russian mob ties, and even though his money was safe, that didn't mean he was.

"After Vann went on his spree, it kicked everyone into high alert," Con said. "Now, we just have to beat Harry at his own game."

"I shouldn't have dragged you into this."

Con snorted. "Dragged? Let's not get crazy."

"Stop thinking about how you think you fucked up. Because that's not true. When it was the right time for Vann's move, he made it. Your chess pieces are still on the board," Con told him fiercely.

He looked at Con and yes, the guy knew what he was talking about. Harry might've upped the ante, but Aleks? He was built to win.

Chapter Eight

Aleks spent the next several days working and researching. Brogan was still in the UK for several more days, so Aleks had no distractions, no excuses.

He hated that he found himself counting down the days until Brogan returned, that he looked forward to the man's texts the way he did.

He'd looked up the accident that had killed Brogan's parents and noted with interest that at first the investigation focused on foul play. There was still some doubt as to what truly happened, but it appeared the Montgomery-Johnstones had begged for privacy to mourn. Brogan had been too young to demand further investigation.

Aleks pressed on nightly, doing some private and protected searches on Brogan's family, the business and his real estate ventures. The latter were public information, and a few keystrokes listed the properties he'd owned.

He'd done the same thing for Harry, even going so far as to cross-reference gyms in the area with Harry's holdings in shell companies. Harry owned two gyms well outside the city—one on the border of the next state, and neither were connected to his name at all.

He'd been so busy looking out for Brogan and checking up on the shell companies Harry appeared to have set up in his name that he missed the most obvious of listings. And that night, the same night Brogan was due home, that listing caught Aleks's eye. He pushed his chair away from the desk, not wanting to see what he'd seen, not wanting to deal with what was on the screen.

But he forced himself back to his seat and his eyes on the screen. The property listing sounded familiar. Even so, Aleks hesitated before he mapped the address…and used the street view option.

He stared at the sign on the building. *Iron Eagle Boxing.* A boxing gym. And this wasn't a rental property. When he cross-referenced the name of the gym, the owner was Brogan Montgomery-Johnstone.

Brogan owned a fucking *boxing* gym, just like the kinds guys were recruited from for illegal underground fighting.

Brogan's gym. Not Harry's.

Fuck. There was no way. Had Brogan been playing him this whole time?

Had Aleks been allowing himself to wear blinders?

After two days of ignoring Brogan's calls—because he knew he wouldn't be able to let go of the anger despite the fact that Aleks had found zero evidence connecting Brogan and his gym to the fights—there was a knock on his apartment door.

Dammit.

Aleks thought about not letting him in. But now was the time for serious recon. If Brogan was playing him? Aleks would be broken. But he'd come out of it alive.

It was more than he could say for Brogan.

Aleks looked pissed. It wasn't exactly the greeting Brogan had expected after not seeing him for a week, but then again, nothing good could come from Aleks ignoring his calls. He'd seen Aleks and his many moods over the past weeks—the guy was as mercurial as anything. It was one of the many reasons Brogan was attracted to him.

Brogan decided a wide berth was necessary. He knew how to relax Aleks but he needed to get a read on exactly what was going on inside his head. "Did you just get off work?"

Aleks glanced over Brogan's shoulder and then directly at Brogan. "Shitty day all around."

Brogan leaned against the doorjamb since he still hadn't been invited inside. "Hungry?"

"Not especially."

"Do I need to get you naked?"

"I need to work out."

Brogan smiled. "I've got just the place."

Aleks stared at him. "Didn't you just get off a plane?"

"I slept. Plus it'll take me a few days to catch up from jet lag. Come on." He motioned with his head and Aleks nodded and walked away from the door to grab his keys and wallet and phone.

Welcome back, Brogan. How was your trip?

He sighed inwardly. *What were you expecting, for Aleks to say how much he missed you?*

Well hell, anything would be nicer than the death glare he'd been on the receiving end of.

Aleks got into Brogan's SUV and they drove across town in silence, save for the radio. He had a feeling Brogan was going to take him to X, so he'd been surprised when he'd noted that Brogan was taking him to his gym.

What were the odds? Was Brogan somehow monitoring any searches on his gym and managed to trace it back to Aleks?

When they pulled up to the gym, Brogan pointed. "We're going in there."

"It's closed."

"Unless you've got keys. Come on. This is a good place to work off some steam. After the board of directors meetings, I could use it." Brogan got out and Aleks followed him. "I was planning on coming here before I came to you, but I'm glad it worked out this way."

Aleks couldn't add "me too" so he watched Brogan opening the locks. "You work out here?"

"As often as I can." Brogan opened the door and held it open for Aleks to go in first. "It's my place."

Aleks walked inside slowly, his entire body tense as fuck as he waited for the trap. "Funny, I took you more for the 'big buildings with your name on it' type."

When Brogan didn't say anything, Aleks turned.

"No, you didn't. So let's find out what the hell crawled in your ass so I can take it out and get in there instead." Brogan shut the door, locked it and flipped the lights on.

Aleks started at the empty gym, unwilling to be relieved. Not yet. "Why a gym?"

Brogan shrugged. "Lot of vets in the area with anger management and PTSD issues. Figured a reduced fee and a place to blow off steam in a place that didn't look like a therapist's office was a plus."

Aleks nodded. "That's cool."

"I don't get here as much as I'd like." Brogan pointed. "I've got extra shorts and shirts in the back. Brand-new stuff—let's go change."

Again, Aleks tensed but Brogan led the way…into a clean changing area stocked with towels and tape and gauze. He opened a few cabinets and pulled out clothes for both of them. They changed quickly, or at least Aleks did, wanting to avoid looking at Brogan naked and losing his resolve.

So far, it appeared that Brogan's gym was on the up and up, despite the trail that said otherwise. Which meant that Harry might be setting Brogan up.

And that pissed Aleks off. He took his frustrations out on the man in front of him, sparring, punching, ducking and weaving…but anger wasn't the best mood to fight in. He made mistakes—stupid ones that got him clipped more often than he'd like.

On top of that, Brogan was good. A military man had to fight for his life. Granted, in a different way than Aleks had, but a fight for life was a fight for life. It added an edge to everything a man did, and that was certainly the case for both Brogan and himself. They were well matched.

They didn't let each other off the hook easily. Their punches hurt each other. And neither man held back.

And when one of Brogan's punches sent him reeling, Aleks retaliated by ripping his gloves off and pushing toward Brogan, who caught him by the biceps. They were both already breathing hard, slick with sweat.

Aleks went to pull back but Brogan used an effective move—the military bastard—that took Aleks down and put him flat on his back on the mat.

"Good thing you like this position, because you find yourself in it often enough with me," Brogan told him.

"You fall for it every time," Aleks pointed out and Brogan laughed, then leaned in and bit Aleks's shoulder. "Yeah. Harder."

"Good thing we're alone. Because I wouldn't be stopping even if we had an audience," Brogan warned, then leaned in to kiss him.

Aleks wound himself around Brogan, wondering why he didn't need the same level of pain he usually did to deal with sex.

Because *Brogan*.

Yes, the answer was the two-hundred-plus-pound man on top of him, grinding their pelvises together in a rhythm that made Aleks want to come in his pants like he was a kid.

"Brogan," he heard himself whisper, had no idea what he would've said if Brogan hadn't yanked both their shorts down and slapped their cocks together.

"Yes, baby. Call my name."

"Christ…"

"Close, but I'll take it." Brogan smiled, and why did the guy have to look like a fucking angel?

Wasn't his life fucked enough?

He hadn't asked for rescuing. He'd learned a long time ago that rescuing himself was the best way out.

Rescuing others? He'd tried.

Failed.

What makes you think Brogan needs saving? And if he does, what makes you think you could save Brogan?

He didn't have an answer for any of that. He just knew he couldn't *not* try.

And through all of that thought, Brogan held him down, fucked him, refused to break eye contact, and no matter how badly Aleks wanted to, he couldn't look away. Feelings flooded him and he knew he'd let all of this go too far. There was no turning back.

The problem was he didn't know which direction forward actually *was*.

"Are you going back to X anytime soon?" Brogan asked as they lay on the mat, unable, unwilling to move or get dressed.

Aleks stared at Brogan. "Do I need to?"

Brogan's smile alone could break him. "You already know where I live."

Aleks studied him. "I imagine you're pretty full up."

"On dates? Casual sex? Subs?" Brogan shook his head.

"Ass is everywhere. But I've been interested in you for a long time. And just a taste? It only whet my appetite for more. I enjoyed the fantasy but the real thing? I'm enjoying it a hell of a lot more."

Brogan's words were more effective than a slam to the solar plexus—surprisingly painful and a just-good-enough kind of "hurts so good" hurt to make Aleks realize that he'd made the right decision.

Chapter Nine

Aleks monitored Brogan's accounts as well as his own. And as much as he'd been expecting Brogan to run a background check on him at some point, when he saw that it had been done, he lost it.

The check hadn't caught any of Aleks's buried accounts— he'd set it up purposely that way. What Brogan's people found was exactly what Aleks wanted them to see. Nothing more, nothing less.

It changed *nothing*. Brogan was still at risk because of Harry. Aleks's plan hadn't changed. But something about Brogan checking up on him like he was a fucking street urchin brought out something dark and ugly inside him. Something he couldn't hold back or keep buried.

Here he was, trying to figure out if he needed to keep himself safe from Brogan or just keep Brogan safe, and Brogan was monitoring his precious money…as his cousin seemed to be continually ripping him off.

It didn't matter that Brogan might not know that. Because how could Brogan not know what his cousin *was*?

Instead of calling first, he took a chance that Brogan would be home. Sure enough, security rang Brogan at the same time they waved Aleks up with no problem.

I guess they know the results of the background check too.

By the time the elevator reached the penthouse, Aleks knew two things for sure: he shouldn't have come here this angry, and there was no going back.

When the doors opened, Brogan was rounding the corner from his bedroom, wearing sweats and a T-shirt and a half smile. "Hey—"

"I hear I passed the background test," Aleks said bluntly, holding a palm against the elevator door.

Brogan frowned. "It's standard operating procedure."

Aleks laughed sharply, a bitter sound that made Brogan wince. "You think I'm after your money."

"That's not it."

"Of course it is." Aleks manhandled him up against the wall. "I don't need your goddamned money."

"I know that."

"No, you don't. You don't get it. I don't need your goddamned money because I've got a fucking fortune of my own." Brogan's face—the surprise—convinced Aleks he knew nothing. "That's right, babe. Could buy my own building and slap my name on it if I wanted to. Guess maybe I should be running a security check on *you*."

"Are you done making me feel like shit?" Brogan was furious, as furious as Aleks had been moments earlier, but it wasn't as satisfying as he'd thought. "Get the fuck out."

Yeah, Brogan had been wrong but Aleks had blindsided him. Pushed him way too far. A psychologist would have a field day saying that Aleks had done it on purpose, driven Brogan away, separated himself from Brogan so Aleks could do what needed to be done, guilt-free.

Good job, Aleks. Playing field's all clear...and you're all alone. Again.

Con stared at him, probably because Aleks all but stormed into work the next morning, grunting at hellos. Becca wisely took off for the back, leaving him alone with Quinn and Con.

"You all right, Aleks?" Quinn asked.

"No."

Con narrowed his eyes. "Brogan?"

"It's over," Aleks said shortly.

Con sighed. "Wait, you broke up? Great. Now we'll lose the lease on the place." Aleks didn't answer him, but he had to admit that Con was playing his part to a T, not giving away a hint that they were working together. "Kid, that's why you don't shit where you eat."

"Con, he's going to throw you through a wall if you keep going," Quinn warned. "If you want it rough, come upstairs."

Con stared at Aleks, then raised his brows and looked at Quinn. "Sounds good to me."

For the next several days, Aleks steered clear of Con because he didn't want to have to deal with any of it. He continued checking to make sure no one ran any security or credit checks on his secret accounts. Either Brogan's PI was the easiest guy in the world to fool or Brogan hadn't wanted him to dig very hard.

Dammit, he hadn't expected to miss Brogan as much as he did. And for the first time, that feeling overrode the intense need for vengeance.

The need was still *there* but the all-consuming aspects of it were just fucking crushed and buried by his unrelenting thoughts of Brogan.

So get him back.

"Or get over him," he ground out to himself.

Harry was still out of the country. Aleks couldn't risk a trip to kill him, was still playing the waiting game. Con was working on the lists.

And you're sitting here like a bitch.

He found himself at Club X. He'd spotted Brogan's car, and when he didn't see Brogan at the bar, the bartender took pity on him—or maybe the guy was a true masochist himself—because he told Aleks, "Brogan's in room three. With someone."

With *someone.*

Brogan had probably been with other *someones* during the time he'd been fucking Aleks. They weren't attached at the hip, never discussed monogamy.

Christ, Aleks wanted to shoot himself for even thinking about that shit. How turned around was he?

Why the hell was he so worked up?

His urge to walk out of the club was strong. The urge to break down the door of room three?

Stronger.

But the damned door wasn't even locked, so he didn't have to kick it in, which meant the anger had no edge off it when he walked in and saw Brogan whipping the sub who was shackled to the Saint Andrew's Cross.

The sub was blindfolded, but his head still whipped toward Aleks's direction, the same way Brogan's did.

Aleks was going to say something like, "Guess you're not wasting any time," but something stopped him. Because two could play at this game, and if nothing else, Aleks had mastered strategy. "Sorry, man. Wrong room. I was looking for—"

"Me." The big, bald, muscled Dom from the first night Aleks had met Brogan at the bar came up behind him like a godsend.

And he didn't want to do this with the Dom, but he recognized the save and let the bigger man lead him, with a hand on the back of Aleks's neck, to a room down the hall.

When he closed the door behind Aleks, he said, "Hope I didn't overstep. I just figured you might need help saving face. I'm Callum."

"Aleks. And yeah, I did. Thanks." Aleks stared at him. He was handsome, and at any other time he'd be stripping and fucking without a second though. What the fuck had Brogan done to him? Because Aleks had never had this problem before, had never dealt with this bonding shit. "Christ, this sucks."

Callum laughed.

"Shit, didn't mean you," Aleks told him quickly.

"I know." He looked toward the door. "I don't think your guy's going to stay away too long."

Aleks barely had time to say, "He's not my guy," when Callum closed in on him, pressing him to the wall. The door slammed open and Callum murmured, "Make it look good," before he brought his mouth down on Aleks's.

"Get the fuck off him," Aleks heard Brogan say, his tone even and calm but the undercurrent of anger unmistakable.

"Why's that?" Callum asked.

"He's mine."

At Brogan's words, Aleks's gut tightened in a funny way.

The man leaning against him stayed in place but looked over his shoulder at Brogan. "Funny, but you seemed too busy for him a few minutes ago."

"I wasn't touching the guy I was with."

"Right. Because whipping someone's definitely not intimate at all." He turned back to assess Aleks, then mouthed, "You okay?"

Aleks nodded. Callum pushed away and turned to Brogan. "If he's really yours, you owe him a hell of an apology."

"Right," Brogan said dryly.

Callum turned to wink at Aleks before he left, shutting the door behind him. Aleks remained against the wall, trying to look bored when really his heart was racing. "Nice touch with the 'he's mine' crap. I'm betting you get a lot of ass that way."

Brogan didn't say anything, continued walking until he was inches from Aleks.

Aleks managed, "Don't you have someone you've got to get back to?" as Brogan put his palms against the wall on each side of Aleks's shoulders.

"Why are you here, Aleks?" Brogan asked finally.

Yes, why, *Aleks?* He had a few options—he could tell Brogan to fuck off, because really, Aleks had every fucking right to be mad as hell at him. He could punch the guy. Or he could lean in and kiss him.

He leaned in. Brogan met him halfway.

Option C for the win. The rest of it melted away as Brogan's tongue stroked his. Aleks groaned into his mouth as Brogan's body made contact, pressed his. Aleks wrapped his leg around Brogan, trying to pull him close...impossibly closer.

"Fuck, I missed you," Brogan murmured against his mouth. "I'm—"

"Shut up," Aleks told him, pulling away, not wanting Brogan to apologize for trying to keep himself safe. Aleks should be doing everything in his power to ensure the same. Because for the first time, the thought occurred to him that if Harry didn't value human lives...why would Aleks think he'd treat his cousin any differently? Especially when it came to the family fortune.

Chapter Ten

After Aleks told him to "Shut up," Brogan sucked on the side of his neck, leaving a hot, red swollen spot, and then he did it twice more, needing to mark this man as his, wanted to mark every single open spot of skin he could.

Wanted to brand this man as *his*.

In his mind, Aleks already was. Aleks hadn't admitted it, but the fact that he'd come back and broken into Brogan's session? That spoke volumes.

He walked Aleks backward toward the bed, pushed him down onto it and hovered over him, lowering himself slowly…planning.

Aleks's cock prodded his.

"You and your Dom friend—did you enjoy him kissing you?" He twisted Aleks's nipples, watching Aleks squirm with the mix of pleasure and pain.

"No," Aleks panted as Brogan leaned in and alternately bit and blew on one nipple, then the other. "No!"

"You're sure?" Brogan sucked a nipple hard, pleasuring it as he twisted the other one.

"Yes."

He murmured in Aleks's ear, "Why not?"

After the briefest of pauses, as if he was wrestling with his own thoughts, Aleks burst out with, "Because he wasn't you."

"Good answer, baby. That will get you well fucked tonight."

"Thank fuck," Aleks moaned.

Brogan stripped down and lay on the bed, head on the pillows. Then he handed Aleks a condom. "Put this on me."

Aleks took the condom and rolled it onto Brogan's cock, slowly, a total tease. Brogan bared his teeth but didn't complain.

"Want to fuck you," he said instead.

"Good," Aleks muttered.

He lowered himself onto Brogan's cock slowly and Brogan watched him. When he was buried to the hilt, they both stayed still for a long moment.

Aleks swallowed hard, and then he began to move. "Gonna make it up to you."

"Not…arguing," Brogan managed. Watching Aleks take his cock, riding him, controlling the fuck and making Brogan's head spin…it was the best kind of apology he'd ever had.

Aleks dipped forward, grabbed Brogan's hair and slammed their mouths together, tonguing, tasting. Devouring.

Brogan shuddered, jerked his hips up and groaned. Cursed. His face flushed, his eyes glassed over. He was the one being fucked, but the way Aleks rode him, fast and hard, it was questionable as to who was fucking who. "Faster, baby."

"Still pretending you're in charge?" Aleks panted.

"You know I am." He wound his hand around Aleks's cock and squeezed hard. "You just like my punishments."

Aleks couldn't deny the truth in Brogan's words, so he didn't bother to try. Brogan's eyes were as heady-lidded as Aleks's. Aleks tried to hold on, to retain the control, but his thrusts became erratic as the pleasure intensified, his moans breathless pants as Brogan pulsed inside him, hot and hard. There was no room for anything else between them…nothing but Aleks's lies.

He shoved that out of his mind as he came.

"You didn't put me on the cross," Aleks murmured in the aftermath. He'd reluctantly pulled away from Brogan, took off and tied the condom and then lay down with his cheek against Brogan's chest. Something Brogan hadn't expected but definitely wasn't complaining about.

But now, Aleks lifted his face, his chin balancing on Brogan's chest as Brogan gazed up at his face. "Because you'd hate it."

"How can you know that?"

"Am I right?" he asked and Aleks's eye roll told him he was. "It's more exciting for you to try to hold yourself in place—or have me try to do it. Either way, you get to move. To moan. Tying you up isn't your game. It's not something I'm willing to push to prove dominance."

Aleks gave him a small grin. "Thanks." He lay back down but shifted off to the side a bit so Brogan could stretch.

And with Aleks lying on his side facing him, Brogan traced the tattoos that ran the length of Aleks's right arm, down to the wrist. There was also a tattoo on the back of his hand as well, a phoenix, so finely done. "Did that hurt?"

"They all hurt," Aleks said. "That's part of the draw."

Yes, Brogan could see that. "Which one's your first?"

Aleks seemed to stiffen for a second, like he didn't want to go there, but then he said, "The phoenix."

"Wow. I thought a lot of places refuse to do hands."

"They do. A lot of them won't do hands if it's a first tattoo."

"I guess you convinced someone," Brogan said, tracing the wings with his forefinger.

"Well, I can be pretty damned convincing when I need to be." Especially at eighteen, fresh out of a cage and killing three men. Aleks had looked and acted every bit the wild man he'd become inside. He and Vann stayed together for three months, traveling through the U.S., keeping one step ahead of anyone who might be trailing them. Vann drank and fucked and fought and Aleks did the same, except he'd become drawn to the idea of tattoos. Especially in Russian culture, tattoos had a hell of a lot of meaning. If you knew what to look for, it would take a single glance to know how long someone had been in prison, for what and what his role was in the Russian mafia.

Aleks stumbled upon an old-school Russian tattoo artist in Nevada, of all places, and he'd gone in and perused the photo albums late one night when he hadn't felt like fighting or fucking or drinking.

"You just going to sit on that couch or are you going to book something?" the old man asked, with just enough of a

Russian accent for Aleks to detect.

"Book something," Aleks told him in perfect Russian and watched the man's eyes widen.

After a while, Aleks admitted his family ties, although not the name of his family. There were other ways to prove legitimacy, Aleks had learned early on, and this man Peter knew how to interpret them.

"So did the guy who did this become your mentor?" Brogan asked, pulling him out of his reverie.

That's when Aleks and Vann decided to part ways. Vann was prepping for the military and Aleks couldn't take any more of someone telling him what to do. So when Peter offered to mentor him, Aleks jumped at the chance. "I wasn't sure I'd like it. I didn't think I'd be good at it."

"Why not?"

"You have to be still." After being forced into a confined space for so long, being still was hard for Aleks. In the end, he had to admit the tattooing had been the best thing for that. It soothed him, smoothed out the rough places inside. And it gave him a trade that changed people.

It certainly had changed him.

In the end, he'd told Peter about the deathmatches. Peter hadn't seemed surprised, and if he hadn't been on his deathbed, Aleks might've worried that he'd been made and turned in.

He hadn't needed to. Peter left him the shop, not knowing how much money Aleks actually had access to, but he'd stayed in Nevada for another year after Peter passed, out of respect.

Brogan was watching him carefully, so Aleks turned his

question back to him. "How come you've got none? No one escapes the military without something."

Brogan laughed. "Trust me, it wasn't easy. I can't tell you the amount of times my buddies would drag me along with them to tattoo parlors. In the end, I just sat there and watched them make bad choices."

"You don't have anything you want badly enough to be permanent," Aleks mused. He hadn't meant it as an indictment, but judging by the look on Brogan's face, he'd taken that very personally. And not well.

"Just because I don't want to ink up my body doesn't mean I don't have permanent beliefs," Brogan started.

"Hey, Brogan—I didn't mean—"

"Then what the fuck did you mean, Aleks? Because I'm betting, out of the two of us, I'm not the one with the commitment issues."

Ouch. Okay, then… "You're right, I'm sure. I've never really thought about commitment because I never met anyone I wanted to be committed to."

"Never?" Brogan asked.

"I'm only twenty-six, so don't act like that's so crazy," Aleks pointed out. "One thing I can say is that military guys are really fucking self-righteous."

Brogan raised his brows at that…but he didn't argue. "So, this conversation went downhill fast."

"Better off with sex and not talking," Aleks said. But suddenly, he didn't feel like much of either. Instead, he had a pit in his stomach, from thinking about Peter and his past and tattooing. It was all too fucking much, and truthfully, he was surprised he hadn't had a reaction like this earlier.

Spending time with Brogan should've made him feel like a traitor. It hadn't…until now. "I think I should go."

Brogan rolled onto his back. "Yeah, maybe you should."

Aleks didn't need to hear it twice.

Chapter Eleven

Aleks didn't sleep much that night. He suspected Brogan didn't either but they were both too stubborn to do anything about it.

The next morning, he had an early appointment so he opened the shop, and it was just him and his client—another veteran who was letting Aleks build him a full backpiece. It was intricate and time-consuming and just the kind of work Aleks needed to take his mind off everything else.

After his client left, he headed to the diner for a quick bite. To his non-surprise, Con settled in across from him a few minutes after he'd ordered.

"How're things?" Con asked, and Aleks was too tired to lie.

"We keep fighting."

Con rolled his eyes. "Well yes, I'd expect that. It's your fault."

"How do you know it's my fault?" Aleks demanded.

"Because you're riding a goddamned fine line here. You've got guilt about Brogan but you can't quit him." Con shook his head. "I'm not judging, man, but this is only going to get more difficult."

Aleks finished with work, grabbed his gym bag and took his bike over to Brogan's gym. It was Monday, so the place was shuttered and dark…but not for long.

He got off his bike and dialed Brogan as he walked around toward the back entrance. When Brogan answered with a curt, "What?" Aleks told him, "I need to go to the gym."

Brogan paused and then spat out. "So go to one."

Still pissed. Aleks sighed. "I want to go to yours."

"It's Monday. We're closed."

"I guess I'll have to change that." Aleks hung up as Brogan said "Aleks," in a warning, frustrated tone.

Good. That made two of them. And Aleks had never met a door—or an alarm system—he didn't like. This one was ridiculously simple, especially with the skeleton key Aleks had acquired and kept on his person all the damned time. No one was going to lock him up without a way to escape ever again if he could help it.

His cell flashed in front of his eyes and he pressed his forehead to the cold back door. No triggers. Not now.

He took several deep breaths. It didn't matter if he screwed his eyes shut or kept them open—the images kept coming. Him in the cell. Him fighting.

Him killing…

"Fuck," he muttered. "Can't."

Things got worse and he felt his knees give out. *Fuck.* He held on to the door, fingers scrabbling for something to hold…and then someone was holding him—holding him up with a firm, steady grasp.

"Brogan—"

"Hush." Brogan wrapped a strong arm around him, pressed Aleks's back to his chest and reached past him with the key.

"It's open."

Brogan stared at him hard and then tried the knob. "I suppose you know the code?"

Aleks didn't say anything, let Brogan tug him inside as Brogan hit the buttons to stop the alarm buzzing.

Then he shut the door and maneuvered Aleks against it. "You okay?"

"I am now."

"God, could you come up with a cheesier line?" Brogan muttered, but he looked pleased, despite himself.

"Give me some time." Aleks stared at him and the images of the cages mercifully faded away. "You're too fucking sensitive."

"*I'm* too sensitive?"

"A guilty conscience always jumps."

"Are you trying to start another fight?" Brogan demanded.

Was he? He still wasn't himself—he was shaky, his pulse pounded and his head ached. Part of him just wanted to run, but he wanted Brogan to not let him.

And yes, Con had been right. About everything. *I'll figure it out*, he promised himself. "I came here to fight, but not like that."

"Let me help." He untucked Aleks's shirt and pulled it over his head. Aleks stared at him, unsure…and not minding it.

Brogan ran a single finger along his chin and down his

throat, lingering on his Adam's apple and then again at the hollow where throat met collarbone. Aleks put his head back, baring his throat in a show of submission, knowing exactly what Brogan wanted from him now.

He could kill me now, but he won't.

Aleks knew it with a certainty that made everything come into sharper focus. He let Brogan tug him with a couple of fingers hooked in the front of his jeans. They walked through the darkened gym, with Brogan turning on a couple of lights but not all, and got them onto the mat.

Aleks slid under the ropes and stayed with his back on the mat. Brogan nodded, leaned over him, put his mouth along Aleks's collarbone and sucked a path along his chest, leaving red, swollen markings, teeth marks, a wet trail all the way down Aleks's belly.

Brutal. Motherfucking brutal, and Aleks loved every second of it. By the time Brogan got to his cock, Aleks was straining upward.

"Still," Brogan commanded, and even though Aleks bared his teeth and growled at him, this was the only place and the only time he'd obey. And finally, Brogan sat up and told Aleks to "Roll over." Aleks obliged and Brogan murmured, "Gonna ride you like a horse."

"Any way you want as long as you hurry up and fuck me," Aleks growled, throwing an intense stare over his shoulder.

"Impatient."

"Have we met? Yes, very."

Brogan slapped his ass—once, then twice, nice and hard and Aleks let out a groan and hung his head. "We've met. You think you'll get away with the crap you pulled tonight?"

"Yes," Aleks gasped as Brogan entered him, sliding steadily to the hilt without stopping.

"Keep dreaming." He leaned over and bit the back of Aleks's neck, holding him in place like a wild horse might, while remaining deep inside him, shifting just enough to hit Aleks's prostate and drive him crazy.

Brogan pressed his face to Aleks's shoulder as Brogan manipulated him, pushing his own hips up to drive more deeply inside.

"Good, Aleks…good boy."

"Harder, daddy," Aleks murmured and that made Brogan ultimately lose it. He slammed up into Aleks, which caused Aleks to come immediately, yelling Brogan's name and coming all over his chest and the mat below. "Fucking trying to kill me."

"Your fault with the daddy shit," Brogan groaned.

"I'll take full responsibility. Told you that you had a daddy kink."

"*I* have the daddy kink? Rethink yourself, boy."

Aleks laughed softly. They were both still panting—and Brogan was still inside him when he told Aleks, "I want to take this to the next level."

Aleks turned to stare over his shoulder at him. "The gym?"

"Are you really that good at playing an asshole or are you really one?"

"You seem to know me so well, why don't you—"

Brogan cut him off mid-sentence, and Aleks suddenly found himself flipped over and flat on his back with Brogan's palm across his throat. Not a killer one—a dominance hold. "I want to be exclusive. With you."

Aleks's gut tightened. "Moving fast."

"You seeing a lot of other guys on the side?"

"Are you?"

Brogan rolled his eyes. "No. I'm only seeing you. I've got no interest in seeing anyone else."

"Okay."

"Okay to…?"

"You really want to go that far?" Aleks asked. "You sure?"

"Very," Brogan said seriously.

Aleks reached up and ran his knuckles along Brogan's jawline, even as Brogan's hand remained on his throat. "I've never done this."

"Fucked in a gym?"

"Thought about committing to someone."

"I know. Seems fast, but…"

"Ten years."

"Ten years," Aleks repeated. "Guess we made a big impression on each other."

"I guess so."

Aleks's belly tightened. "I hated to fight."

"I figured that out."

"When?"

"The first night we fucked and you asked if I wanted to pay you. I hate that you think—"

"You don't know what I think."

"I'm not a rich asshole with nothing better to do than buy his way through men."

Aleks stared at him. Nodded. And thankfully, Brogan didn't press it any further, just tugged him closer.

"My wild thing," Brogan murmured against his ear.

Aleks jerked a little. "What did you call me?"

"Mine," Brogan told him.

Aleks turned to stare up at him with an expression Brogan couldn't read on his face. "I've never...done this. Been with anyone. Not like this."

Brogan stroked his hair. "How's it feel?"

"I don't know."

"You're still here."

"I guess that speaks more than words," Aleks muttered, almost sounding angry with himself.

"Want to stay at my place?" Brogan asked as he locked up the gym and they walked to their respective car and bike.

"I've got to work early," Aleks said.

"Tomorrow night, then?" Brogan asked.

"I'll call you."

Brogan frowned a little but then changed tactics. "So, how do you feel about coming to a wedding?"

It was Aleks's turn to frown. "Now you're definitely moving too fast."

"Yeah, don't flatter yourself. It's my cousin, Harry."

Aleks's gut twisted. "When is it?"

"Next month. It's very sudden. He's always been impulsive, but this? His mom—my aunt—she's flipping out trying to put together a formal wedding in a month."

"Harry and his bride-to-be aren't helping?"

"Are you kidding? They're traveling. He's used to having everything done for him and his fiancée is the same way. I'm not sure my aunt's even told them their wedding date."

"So your aunt's cool with this—with you inviting me?"

"She was the first one who knew I was gay—probably around the same time I figured it out."

"Okay, then." He'd have to take out Harry before that, but at least he had a date when Harry would be back in the States. Unless... "Destination wedding?"

"Are you kidding? There's a church named after us. The Montgomery-Johnstones all get married there. And it's right in town."

And there it was, just like Aleks knew would happen—the perfect opportunity at the most imperfect time.

"Hey." Brogan looked concerned. "You all right?"

"I'm fine. Perfect," Aleks lied. Because that was the best thing he could do for Brogan right now. Maybe it was all he could ever do.

Chapter Twelve

Con got the list. All told it had taken the better part of a month, during which Harry continued traveling through Europe, and Brogan attended several meetings in London with the Montgomery-Johnstone board of directors. But finally, the ring shaped up enough to formalize their list of recruits and their targets.

It made Aleks sick to look at.

"You've got a window of maybe a week before they start going over these people," Con told him, his voice low, even though they were safely in Aleks's apartment. Aleks understood—when this shit started happening, it seemed like no place was safe. "I could warn the fighters but one of them will sing."

Con was right. Harry needed to go down. "A week sounds about right. The wedding's this Sunday. I'd imagine he's got to touch down here at the very least the night before," he managed, his voice sounding calmer than he felt.

Con leaned forward, put a hand on his arm. "Listen to me, Aleks—I'll do this for you. Gladly. Just say the word. I've got nothing to lose killing Harry. My conscience will be clean."

But Aleks shook his head. "Mine would be too."

"You'll be sleeping in bed next to his cousin every night. I don't consider that clean," Con reasoned.

"It's my responsibility. It's for my brother. If I can't live with it…"

"Okay, man, I get it." Con took a deep breath. "I'll keep up my part in this until you tell me otherwise."

Aleks nodded, grateful that Con would trust him. Now, more than ever, Aleks needed to assess Brogan's involvement… and let Brogan know what was going to happen. It was put up or shut up time, and Aleks was prepared to do whatever it took to keep his end of the bargain to Vann and to Brogan.

Aleks went over it in his head as he hit the bag with brute force.

You're going to kill his cousin to save his life…when you don't know if his life needs saving.

Or you could tell him. Everything.

Right, like Brogan would just say, "Okay, great, go ahead and kill Harry and we'll live happily ever after."

"Motherfucker!" he roared and kicked the bag, hard enough to bend the metal bar it hung from. He stopped, hung his head.

He owed it to himself and Vann to carry out the original plan. Harry Montgomery-Johnstone deserved nothing less than death, and probably a harsher one than he'd get. If it meant Aleks had to sacrifice his happiness for that, he would. His brother deserved nothing less.

"Sorry—can't tonight," Aleks told Brogan for the third night in a row.

"Or any night this week. Aleks, I'm a big boy—"

"So then deal with it," Aleks snapped.

"I'm coming in."

"What the fuck?" Aleks glanced at his door out of habit… just in time to see Brogan letting himself in. "Seriously. What the fuck?"

"You think you're the only one who can break into places?" Brogan looked entirely too smug as he locked the door behind him.

Aleks waited for Brogan to walk over to him, his heart pounding. He knew what he should do—tell Brogan everything, tell him to walk away and then Aleks would carry out his plan.

He knew what he wanted to do in this very moment. Because if it was between talk or sex, sex was easier, and harder, in many respects. But Aleks could handle that kind of invasion from Brogan. Probably even needed it. "Your place," he managed.

Brogan stood inches from him, watching him carefully. "Okay. But we'll talk after," he said, as though reading Aleks's mind.

Aleks only nodded and let Brogan steer him out of the apartment and into his car. The ride was a silent blur. Brogan parked in the familiar garage, and the men kept their hands to themselves in the elevator.

Aleks wasn't sure why he was so drawn to Brogan's place, why it was important to be here instead of his place when they talked… he just knew it was.

"Enough thinking," Brogan told him. "Bedroom."

Aleks followed him after toeing off his heavy boots and leaving them by the door. He put his wallet, phone and keys there too, like he was unconsciously planning a quick escape, and it didn't go unnoticed by Brogan, who merely looked at what Aleks had done and frowned a little.

But Aleks did what he'd asked, went into the bedroom and stripped.

"On all fours, facing the headboard."

Aleks followed Brogan's orders, loving it and hating it at the same time.

Brogan shoved Aleks's face down into the pillow, twisting his hands in Aleks's hair, telling him to "Stay."

Aleks didn't have much of a choice, since Brogan was currently tying his hands behind his back—more of a symbolic gesture than a hard hold but it was still way fucking hotter than Aleks would've thought—and then hoisted his hips up, forcing him onto his knees, shoulders touching the mattress.

Brogan slapped Aleks's ass, several times, leaving satisfying red marks on and hearing the even more satisfying moans that drummed up from Aleks's throat.

"Beautiful. I like you like this, not talking back, unable to do anything but shut up and take the pleasure I give you."

Aleks rumbled something deep in his chest (cursing at Brogan, no doubt) but Brogan didn't care. He wanted Aleks on sensory overload, wanted to turn him into a shaking, panting, goddamned mess of a man.

He knew he was close when he heard Aleks murmuring something in Russian. He couldn't understand it but could recognize the language. Maybe Aleks didn't realize he was doing it at all. Brogan tried to commit a few of the phrases or at least some of the words to memory so he could look them up later.

"So...the Russian?" he murmured and Aleks turned his head to stare at him, his dark eyes searching Brogan's, and although his expression didn't change, his body tensed.

"It slips out sometimes."

"Only sometimes."

"When I forget," he explained. "It slips out when I let myself forget."

"Forget more," Brogan murmured.

Aleks gave a stuttered laugh but didn't answer. Brogan steadied his body over Aleks's, wanting to hear that again, wanting Aleks to forget and lose himself.

Wanted all of him, in the most selfish ways possible. Brogan would take the unwilling man under him and make him beg for it.

And Brogan put his hand flat in the middle of his back, pressing his shoulders to the mattress, forcing his forehead to do the same again, ass up in a seemingly humiliating position, knees spread, Brogan blowing on his hole, making it twitch and Aleks squirm.

Aleks huffed, "Fuck...you're not going to..." right before Brogan's tongue flattened against the spot that made Aleks cry out in a howl, even as his cheeks flushed hot and he buried his face in the pillow and moaned like a bitch.

Brogan buried his face in Aleks's ass and ate it until Aleks was straining the sheets, crying out and cursing, unable to move away from Brogan's machinations.

When his tongue was replaced by his cock, he kept pressing Aleks's back, and with a hard push, he entered him, splitting him, filling him and then fucking him as hard as he could…talking Aleks for a wild ride.

And Aleks had been muttering again, in Russian, the words pouring out of him.

"You like being pounded."

"Fuck, yes."

"By me."

"Yes."

"Opening up to me. Being held down by me."

"Yes," Aleks ground out. "Yes to all of it. Now let me come."

Brogan hit his prostate three times in quick succession and Aleks froze, muscles taut as a bow pulling back before he shot, balls tightening like he was blowing his load through a cannon.

Aleks's orgasm seemed to last forever—longest one he could ever remember, like it was several rolled into one… and then everything was white and hazy and perfect.

At some point, he realized his legs were trembling. He was vaguely aware of Brogan helping to lower him flat to the bed, groaning as he eased his aching body against the cold sheets. Didn't give a shit about the wet spot, but there wasn't one. Brogan had shoved a towel under them and took it away before Aleks lay down.

Brogan stroked his damp hair now, and the back of his neck as he came down from something pretty damned close to subspace. He lay there, unwilling, unable to look at Brogan. Everything was spiraling. He was spiraling, so far out of control, away from the promises he'd made to himself, to Brad and Vann.

Brogan was wiping him down—all that aftercare bullshit that Aleks hadn't truly understood or appreciated…until now.

The cloth was a perfect temperature, cool but not cold, and it wiped away the sweat. He stared up at Brogan and saw his expression—it was different. Something had happened, and Aleks was as shaken as Brogan was, for different reasons— and one very similar one. That fuck had gone way beyond sex, moved them into a space that there was no coming back from… They could tiptoe away from it, back up slightly. Ignore it. But was there. It happened…and for a moment in time, they both acknowledged it.

When the chill set in, Brogan pulled the blanket over his bare skin. His limbs were lead, his mind floated and he closed his eyes and for the first time he could remember, he slept a dreamless sleep.

Chapter Thirteen

"You've only been out an hour" were Brogan's first words to him when Aleks's eyes opened with a *Where the fuck am I?* start.

"Christ," he muttered. "That was…" Amazing. Intense. *Everything.*

Brogan smiled a little. "I loved seeing you like that. Like this. I love seeing you any way you are, Aleks. You have to know that."

Aleks realized he did. He never would've seen Brogan again after the first night if he could've helped it.

"Aleks, what's going on?" Brogan pressed quietly.

Aleks stared up at him. "Really? You're doing this now when I'm helpless?"

Brogan snorted softly. "You're never helpless." But then he frowned, and maybe Aleks's expression gave too much away, letting Brogan know that he'd been wrong about Aleks's helplessness.

Aleks hesitated and then said, "I meant it when I said okay…about our commitment. But then I started thinking."

"And what did you come up with?"

"You fell in lust, Brogan."

Brogan nodded slowly. "At first, sure. But lust doesn't usually last for this long."

"It's fantasy," Aleks insisted.

"But this…" Brogan motioned between the two of them. "Isn't. It's flesh and blood."

"Right. Which is why it won't work."

"You need to explain," he demanded. "Because right now, I'm not sure which one of us you're trying to convince."

"Because now that I'm real, it's real…"

"Makes it better," Brogan said firmly.

"Fantasy's easier."

"Yes, but not as fulfilling. I told you, it's about more than fantasy. Because even though I didn't meet you that night at the fight…we connected. I don't know why. I was struggling, going against my family. I was headed into a hard-as-fuck training program and maybe I saw something in you that could save me. Maybe your strength gave me a lifeline."

"Maybe I was drowning too," Aleks managed.

"Then tell me. Tell me everything. I want to know," Brogan urged.

"No, you don't. And I couldn't anyway."

Brogan stared at him. "I'll wait, Aleks. You can't deny there's something between us. In fact, you wouldn't be fighting this hard to deny it if you didn't feel it."

Aleks couldn't admit that he was right. Because admitting that would start an avalanche of events that nothing could stop. It was either dig in deeper or cut bait and run.

So he stared at Brogan…and dove in. "The fights…"

"You didn't like them."

"I hated them."

"You needed money."

He laughed, an odd sound in the too-quiet room. "Not for me. I was paying off a debt."

Brogan frowned. "Like a gambling debt?"

"No. And it wasn't just one night." *Rip the fucking Band-Aid off, Aleks.* "Two years. I fought for two years in order to help my brother."

"You brother who died?"

"Yes. And I don't think I want to do this now. Any of it. I don't want to tell you the rest of the story."

"I want to help you."

"But I don't need your fucking help." Aleks's voice shook with exposed, raw anger. His body ached like he'd just fought for his life and he just wanted to put all this behind him.

The fights, the cages…all of it, flashing in picture after picture in front of his eyes until his head felt ready to explode.

For years, he'd had one road, one trail to follow. Revenge was a powerful taskmaster—and a necessary one in this case, but he was being tugged in a direction his heart wanted to go but his head knew he couldn't.

"Did the people you fought for hurt your brother?" Brogan pushed.

Aleks shot to his feet. "They killed him. The fuckers killed him and by doing that, they took a piece of me."

They stared at each other, with Aleks shaking from rage. And instead of asking any more questions, Brogan simply pulled him in close and held him. Wrapped his arms around Aleks hard, a comfort measure, and they remained like that until Aleks felt strong enough to pull back.

When he did, Brogan told him, "I didn't know anything about using fighters to pay off debts. You have to believe that."

"Why? Why the fuck's that so important to you?"

"If they forced you to fight to work off Berdy's debt…that's extortion. I don't support that shit and I sure as hell wouldn't have come to watch you fight under those circumstances."

"Aren't you a Boy Scout."

"I would've shut it down," Brogan said, his voice a fierce growl.

"Why? Because you're a do-gooder?" Aleks pushed him hard and Brogan stumbled back a step but caught himself quickly. Aleks was in his face just as fast. "You don't know what the fuck you're doing. Stay out of it."

"Really? Why's that? Because you had so much fun there?"

"I wasn't there against my will. It doesn't work like that," Aleks hissed.

"Then tell me what it's like," Brogan demanded. "Because right now, you're so goddamned turned around that you think you went there to fight out of your own free will. Nothing about what you were pushed to do was consensual, Aleks, no matter what they tried to make you believe. You were coerced. And none of this was your fault."

Brogan braced himself for another push, but instead Aleks took a step back and muttered, "Fuck," his expression flashing to that angry one Brogan remembered so well. It hadn't been an act, that edge of crazy Aleks brought to the ring. "I did it to save my brother. I had no other choice—no money, so I bartered the only thing I had. Myself."

Brogan sighed. Looked at the ceiling. "Shit. Aleks, I can't believe—"

"Of course you can't. You were there, paying for it. Enjoying it. Yelling for the winner," Aleks bit out. "None of you or the other men who paid to watch me fight had any thoughts about why we were doing it." Aleks laughed, an almost hysterical sound. "Yes, I turned myself over to the cage most willingly. Because I had to work off the debt to save my brother from the cage they put him in."

"Wait, what?" Brogan had gone still. Dangerously so.

"The men who ran the ring kidnapped my brother, then sent for me. And they gave me a reasonable choice—fight for them and I could have my brother back, or walk away and they'd kill him immediately." Aleks's tone was flat but there was fire in his eyes. "I guess you know which one I chose."

"Caged. They caged both of you...for years," Brogan repeated slowly, because he needed to hear himself say it out loud, even as his gut contracted with the horror of what Aleks had unfolded for him. The horror that Aleks lived with for years...the horror he could barely admit actually happened. And then Brogan was babbling, trying to scrabble for the right words...and knowing when they came out that they were all wrong. "I knew it wasn't a legal ring—underground fighting never is, but that..."

"Right. I lost my brother and you're worried you were in more of an illegal than normal underground fighting space."

He grabbed Aleks by the shoulders. "That's not what I mean and you fucking know it."

"No, I don't know anything except you paid money and watched me fight." Aleks jerked away. "Those were the early matches. The 'fun' ones. They tended to get a little dark toward the end."

"Dark how?'

"Well, I'm not sure you'd have had the same hard on watching me strangle my opponent to death. Then again, maybe you're into that shit."

Brogan's head spun. "I can't believe this. I can't fucking believe it."

"How should I convince you?" Aleks asked dryly.

"Did he know?"

"Did who know?"

"Harry—did he know?"

Aleks shrugged but Brogan had his answer. Then Aleks asked, "Did *you* know?"

That stopped Brogan cold. "Are you asking if I knew what the ring was all about?"

"Yeah, that's what I'm asking."

"Have you been with me this entire time wondering if I was in on you living in a cage, forced to kill men to save your brother?" Brogan demanded.

"Yes."

Brogan turned away, feeling the bile rise in his throat. What kind of man did Aleks think he was? And honestly, how and why would Aleks think differently? "Are you with me because of this, for recon, or in spite of yourself?" he asked, his voice tight, his throat painfully so.

He turned to see Aleks's face when Aleks admitted, "In spite of."

That was the single bright spot of this entire shitshow. "Did you think I came back to the States to find you… that I found out you'd moved here?"

Aleks nodded and Brogan registered that, every time they were together, Aleks wasn't sure if he should be expecting sex or an ambush.

Aleks continued. "See, they fixed it perfectly. They filmed it. Somewhere there's a film of me killing three men. So I don't go to the police, I'm not turned in for a triple homicide." He shrugged. "But I don't plan to let them get away with it. It's been eight years, but I haven't forgotten. If nothing else, I'm a patient fucker."

"Do I want to know what that means?"

"Do you?" Aleks challenged.

"I need you to tell me."

Aleks shook his head. "Figure it out for yourself. I'm done helping your family."

"That's not fair. You're not giving me a chance to make things right."

"Why would you want to do that?" Aleks asked.

"Because I'm falling for you. And if you tell me you haven't realized that, you're lying," Brogan shot back. "I probably started the night I saw you. I haven't been able to stop thinking of you, which now sounds so fucked up, given the circumstances."

"I've thought about you a lot over the years too," Aleks admitted.

"Because you knew who I was?"

"I didn't. Not right away. I didn't start researching anything until a couple of years after I was freed. I didn't want to put any suspicion on myself, in case they were tracking me."

And that's why the security check hit Aleks so hard. That's why all of this had become a push-pull for far more than the commitment issues Aleks had.

Had any of it been real between them? Brogan believed it was, because Aleks could fake a lot of things, but every man's guard was down when he was coming. That's where all the truth spilled out, as it were. And Aleks was no different.

Aleks was careful not to mention Vann at all to Brogan. That was their deal—separate responsibilities and they'd never sell the other out. Brogan was coming to some ugly realizations and even though it would help Aleks walk away in the long run, it was making his chest ache in the short term. "This is something I have to do, Brogan. I get that you want to make things right, but it's not your place to do that."

"Aleks, you really expect me to stand back and let you—"

"Yes." Aleks cut him off. "Walk away and let me take care of my business."

"We're involved." Brogan motioned between them.

"Now you're worried you could get in trouble?"

"I'm worried about you, for a lot of reasons. I don't want anything else on your conscience."

"My conscience is clean," Aleks said furiously. "Walk away, Brogan, the way I'm about to. Walk away, don't look back and don't bother brushing off your tux—you won't need it this weekend. That's all you need to do." Aleks picked up Brogan's cell phone off the table. "Here. Call your cousin. Call and warn him I'm coming. Ease your conscience. It won't matter."

Brogan didn't move, his expression shuttered. "You were just…fuck." Brogan stared at him, his eyes haunted by the realization.

Then he did something that Aleks had never expected. He got on his knees and stared at Aleks as he threaded his fingers together behind his head. "Go ahead, Aleks."

"Why the hell are you doing?"

"You're looking for sacrifices. Revenge."

He had been. He'd thought Brogan could lead him down the perfect path to find vengeance. And then… "No. Get the fuck up."

Brogan remained on his knees, staring up at him. "Why not? It's what you wanted."

"No. Not you."

"But you've been using me to get to Harry."

Tell him that's how it started out, but now everything's different. Tell him that everything's changed.

Instead, Aleks said, "Like I said, you can warn Harry about me, but it won't matter. He'll never see me coming."

Brogan got off his knees in one smooth movement. "Aleks, I'm begging you not to do this—and it has nothing to do with wanting to save Harry. I called him last night. I told him that I'd met you, that I remembered you from the fights. And I told him you were coming to the wedding." Brogan paused as they both absorbed the enormity of what he'd done. "I didn't know—"

"I know that," Aleks said. "And it doesn't matter how ready he might think he is for me."

"Harry deserves whatever he gets, and I'll help you make

sure justice is served. Please—call the police and tell them everything."

Aleks pressed his lips together for a brief second. "Right. The police. Even if Harry didn't have the video, picture me going up against your family, Brogan."

Brogan's expression hardened but he didn't argue. Because he knew exactly what Aleks was talking about—money talked and Aleks had no proof of what had happened to him. "There's got to be something I can do."

"You can probably testify against me. You saw me fighting illegally. And everything I've told you—I've got no proof, except my word and Berdy's death. They'll say I'd do anything to save my own ass, and I know that's exactly what it looks like." He didn't want to do this, not to Brogan. Not to either of them. But he had to drop the guillotine and deliver possibly the most cutting blow in all of this. "And they'll paint you as trying to oust your cousin from the business, because that's the trail Harry set up to frame you. If I do go to the police… all signs point to you being the guilty one. And if you go in and check on the trail, try to change it, it will make you look guiltier. He's set up shell companies for you. You own a gym." He stopped, because it was already so bad, and he didn't want to make it worse. But Brogan needed to understand there was nothing he could do to help. Nothing within the law.

Brogan fisted his hands. "Damn him. Damn him to hell."

"I can't say I don't agree."

"I can handle it. I can prove—"

"No. It doesn't matter. I have my path. I can't say I'm unhappy about the way it veered, but it's made it harder to remain clear on what I need to do. I owe my brother—my family." His voice broke slightly on those last words, so he paused, gathered himself. Then he looked at Brogan and asked hollowly, "You really had no idea?"

"None. Dammit." Brogan paced, then stopped. "What the fuck do you think of me? Of my family?"

"I don't think you want to know that last part."

Brogan looked shattered, like his world was collapsing. "Aleks, please."

"Let me leave, Brogan. Just let me walk out of your apartment—your life—to do what I have to do."

"No. No, no, no!" Brogan shouted. "Don't walk out on me. On us."

Play it, Aleks. "That's bullshit and you know it."

And that doesn't matter. Can't.

Still, he knew Brogan wouldn't let him leave without a fight. But Aleks didn't fight anymore—he put a stop to things. This couldn't be any different.

"Goodbye, Brogan." He reached into the elevator and pulled the fire alarm so it would stop the elevator from functioning, and when Brogan reached out to stop him from using the stairs, Aleks threw a surprise left hook that took Brogan down to the ground, stunning him. Not for long, though—and Aleks paused to make sure that Brogan hadn't hit his head on anything harder than the carpet before he took off down the stairs.

Brogan would be too disoriented to follow very fast, and by the time the elevator stopped ringing, Aleks would be long gone.

He got to his bike just as Brogan burst into the garage and he peeled out of the parking lot before he looked back and lost his resolve.

Chapter Fourteen

Brogan watched as Aleks's bike sped off into the night. Stood there, in the cold, in bare feet, didn't matter. He'd gone numb inside after Aleks had told him about the fights. Wasn't sure he'd ever thaw out again.

"You dumb fuck. Couldn't just play the family game and keep your mouth shut?"

Brogan turned to see Harry, holding a gun. Harry, who he'd made suspicious with his phone call.

"But no," Harry continued. "You had to ruin it by selling out our family. You realize that your money is also tainted—same last name, same money, same funding. I could wash your money if that would help you sleep better at night. But you should know better than to sleep with the help anyway."

Brogan wanted to lunge but Harry was too far away. Advantage, gun. For now.

At least Aleks had gotten away safely. "You're still involved in this shit? In killing people's family members if they don't fight in your club?"

"No worse than big game hunting. It's a novelty. You know

how many new clients we bring in after taking them to the fights? Most people don't realize how bloodthirsty they are until they see bloodshed."

"You think it's about sport? What the hell is wrong with you, Harry?"

He flicked the gun toward his car. "Get in the trunk."

"If I don't?"

Harry snarled. "How worried do you want to be about Aleks? Because I've got someone watching him. You want him alive, you come with me. Now."

Without further argument, Brogan climbed into the trunk. Before Harry shut the door, he slammed Brogan's skull with the butt of the pistol and his world went black.

Aleks went to Inked to find Con. It was pretty busy for a random Thursday night but all the clients were being taken care of. Con and Quinn were behind the desk, talking, and they looked up when he came in.

Both looked concerned, for different reasons. "Hey, Aleks. You look like you need a drink," Con said carefully.

"Let's go next door and grab a few," Quinn suggested.

Aleks should've called Con instead. There was no way he was putting a wedge between the men. "Thanks, but I'm just beat. Needed to check my schedule for tomorrow."

Con nodded and pushed the appointment book toward him, and Aleks studied it like he'd be tested on it. Really, the words swam in front of him, but he ran his finger down the list and nodded a few times like he was recalling things.

Where would he be tomorrow? In jail? On the run? He shook that off and handed Con back the book. "Thanks."

"All planned out?" Con asked, and he wasn't talking about tattoos.

"As always," Aleks told him. But when his phone rang and he saw Harry's name on the caller ID, everything changed. "Back in a sec." He pointed to the phone as he went outside to take the call.

"Yeah?" he asked warily when he picked up.

"Hello, Aleksandr. Remember me? I'm sure you do—you've been stalking me for years."

Harry. Aleks stared at Con through the window of Inked and said, "What do you want, Harry?"

"You. I'm assuming you'd trade yourself for my cousin, considering you two are now an item."

Harry had Brogan? Harry was here? Last time Aleks checked, Harry's flight was still booked for two days from now. If he'd flown, Aleks would've been alerted, which meant Harry had flown under a different name.

Which also meant that Harry had been onto him longer than Aleks realized. Unless Brogan's phone call had made Harry suspicious.

But sometimes an innocent can cause more danger just by being innocent. "If you touch him—if he has so much as a single bruise on him—"

"Fuck you, Aleks. That's my decision. I'll keep him alive for the next hour. The rest is up to you. And by the way—come alone or I'll kill Brogan the second I see one other person with you," Harry warned.

Harry was a man with nothing to lose. He had the perfect

set-up—his cousin was in on illegal schemes and Harry killed him and his lover in self-defense. Aleks refused to pull Con into this. He'd already put him too much at risk. "I'll be there. Alone. Where am I going?"

"You've pulled all the bank statements. Since you know me so well, you'll know exactly where I am. Clock's ticking." Harry hung up and Aleks took a deep breath before sticking his head in the door of Inked and saying, "I've got to run. I'll see you guys tomorrow."

He didn't stick around to see if either man believed him.

Based on what he'd just witnessed, coupled with what he'd been noticing over the past weeks, Quinn now knew definitively that something big was going on between Aleks and Con. Something life or death, if the looks on both Aleks and Con's faces were any indication, and although Quinn had suspected that Con had been working on something above the law, he hadn't been able to figure out what.

Until now.

He motioned for Con to follow him to the back, and Con did. "Close the door," he said and Con complied. And then Quinn crossed his arms and just stared at Con, who squirmed under his interrogation-like gaze.

"Fuck. I can lie to anyone. Why not you?" Con grumbled.

Quinn still glared, ultimately grateful that Con couldn't lie to him.

"I'm helping Aleks," Con finally admitted, far more quickly than he would've under normal circumstances, which meant that Aleks was in trouble.

"Really." Sarcasm dripped from Quinn's delivery. "Care to tell me all about it? Or would you like to keep me in the dark, and not realizing I should be protecting myself or watching your back from imminent danger?"

"When you put it that way, it sounds bad." Con sighed and Quinn glared at him again. "Fine. I'll tell you everything. But trust me, if Aleks had come to you with this shit, you'd have done exactly what I did."

Chapter Fifteen

When Brogan came to, the first person he saw was Aleks. For a few seconds, he had hope that he'd been rescued, that he was in a hospital bed sleeping off a concussion...except...

Harry was there. Watching both of them. And they were in the back room of Brogan's gym. "You shouldn't have come here," he managed to tell Aleks.

"This is my fault, not yours," Aleks told him.

"So sorry to break up this sweet reunion," Harry interrupted. "But I invited Aleks and he came willingly. Just like you, Brogan."

"Fuck off," Aleks muttered.

"Brogan, meet Aleksandr Solonick. You landed yourself a rich Russian boy," Harry said. "Congratulations. But I can't let you walk off into the sunset together."

He'd known all along, the bastard. *Miserable motherfucker.* "It was you who started the fire," Aleks said dully.

"Give the rich Russian boy a prize. Took you this long to figure this out? They told me you were smart. But I turned you into a killer. God, you have no idea what a fucking rush that was. Like being a keeper of some exotic zoo."

Zoo.

Caged.

Animal.

That's all he'd been, all Vann and the others had been to Harry. Sport, pure and simple.

Harry continued, "If my asshole client hadn't opened his mouth, none of this would've happened."

"I would've gotten my brother back?" Aleks asked.

"Sure," Harry said sarcastically. "And you would've gotten a trophy and a dozen roses."

Aleks and Vann were never set to be freed. Maybe they would've been forced into service for much longer, and Aleks didn't want to know what Berdy and Lola had gone through in captivity. Anything he'd come up with in his head was far worse than anything Harry would've told him.

"It didn't matter what you did to me, then. It didn't matter what you planned," Aleks told him now. "You were always a dead man."

"Really? Because you can't fight a gun." Harry glanced at Brogan. "Two of you are really sweet together. Maybe Brogan should fight for you? What do you think, Aleks? Just like old times, except you can sit in a cage and think about Brogan coming to rescue you."

Fuck no. He'd die on the spot rather than let anyone experience the torture he'd been put through.

"Did the Russian mob force you into this?" Brogan

demanded, his pupils blown.

"Force me? I never went to them." Harry looked insulted. "I'd heard about the fights, went and saw one. I decided to invest and to run my own version. Now the Russians? They come to me."

"Jesus Christ. Does our family name mean nothing to you?" Brogan asked.

"Sorry. I'll do some charity shit to make up for my sins," Harry said sarcastically.

"Going to take more than that," Aleks muttered.

"You always did have a smart mouth." Harry stared at him. "I knew I'd let you go for too long."

"You were still in London this morning," Brogan said to Harry.

"I told you I was. You're as naive as ever, Brogan. I thought the military would've given you some balls."

What it had done was let Harry's words not affect Brogan in the least; his expression was stone cold nothing.

In a fight—gym or no gym—Aleks would bet on Brogan. But Brogan wanted to listen to Harry instead, which would fuck him over.

"Your 'friend' here? Did you know he's had a plan to kill me for…how many years is it, Aleks?"

"Eight years," Aleks offered helpfully for Harry while staring at Brogan.

"Didn't he tell you that when he started fucking you to get information?" Harry demanded.

"To be fair, he fucked me. But in a much different way than you did," Aleks said.

"You were going to kill my cousin," Harry said.

Aleks laughed. "I'm going to kill you, Harry. That's all."

"You heard that, Brogan? Your boyfriend betrayed you. Set it up to look like you and I were both in on the fighting ring. He's sick." Harry shook his head.

"Right. He signed himself up for the deathmatches and imprisoned his own brother," Brogan started.

"He was going to *kill us*," Harry emphasized.

"I don't blame him. But now you're going to kill us, right?" He looked over at Aleks than back at Harry. "Do you think I didn't see the accounts?"

Harry frowned—Brogan hadn't seen shit. Aleks knew that, but his tone was authoritative enough to trip Harry up for a few moments.

"Did he tell you he's from a Russian mob family?" Harry shook his head sadly as he came forward with a needle. Aleks froze and Brogan tried to pull away.

"Harry, please—think about this," Brogan managed, as calmly as he could.

"Think about how guilty you'll look either way," he told Brogan as the needle pricked the skin on the left side of his neck. "You think I'm going to wait around? I know Aleks probably has friends coming soon."

He said that, was halfway finished with pressing the plunger when everything went nuts. Brogan's eyes widened and Aleks was behind Harry, had him by the neck in a chokehold. But Harry was reaching for his gun.

With the needle still in his neck, Brogan fought off the

woozy feeling. He held his breath as Aleks wrestled the gun from pointing at Brogan and instead, turned it toward Harry.

"No, Aleks," Brogan whispered, because Aleks was standing directly behind Harry. Because even though Harry would take the impact of the bullet, Aleks wouldn't be able to stop it from ripping through his own body.

"I'm taking him with me," Harry told Brogan.

But Aleks had other ideas. With his bare hands, he held onto both sides of Harry's chin and, with a hard and fast move, he snapped Harry's neck.

Chapter Sixteen

Everything had happened so fast. Aleks let go of Harry's body and reached out to pull the needle carefully from Brogan's neck as the police sirens wailed in the distance. There was a commotion at the door and Aleks picked the gun up and stood in front of Brogan to protect him.

But Con was holding his weapon too and they both immediately lowered them. "Quinn's outside waiting for the police."

"Ambulance," Aleks managed as he turned back to Brogan and pointed. He heard Con yelling for Quinn and told Brogan, "I didn't kill him for any other reason—"

"Than to save me. I know, Aleks. Fuck, I know." Brogan shuddered, the drugs still strong in his system. "What did he give me?"

Aleks didn't want to tell him, wanted to say *I have no idea but you'll be fine.* But he couldn't. "The same drugs he gave my brother."

Brogan exhaled shallowly as Aleks untied him. "Got to get you to a hospital. Not sure how much he gave you but the syringe was only halfway done. That's a good sign."

He didn't want to think about the fact that if he'd taken any longer to get out of the bonds, Brogan would be gone. Instead, he gathered Brogan up as best and gently as he could and carried him up and out of the basement.

"I can walk—"

"And then the shit spreads faster," Aleks told him. Because that's exactly how his sister and Vann's girlfriend had died. Panic made the poison run through their veins faster.

He saw Con and Quinn waving down the police car and he laid Brogan carefully down on the sidewalk, cradling his body against his.

When the officer came over, Aleks told him, "He's been poisoned. Need an ambulance."

"Bus is on the way," the officer confirmed as he took in both men's bloodstained clothes. He looked directly at Aleks. "Sir, I'll need to speak with you."

"As soon as the ambulance comes," Aleks told him.

"Sir—"

The siren cut through the air sharply. Aleks almost collapsed with relief when the EMTs got to Brogan, understood what the syringe that Aleks handed them meant and began the IV before getting him into the ambulance.

"Will it work?" Aleks asked as he picked Brogan up and placed him on the stretcher as the EMTs made sure his lines weren't tangled.

"We won't know yet, but it's the best we can do. We'll get him to the hospital ASAP," the EMT assured him.

"You can't ride with him," the officer told Aleks now. "We have questions for you."

"I'll go with him," Quinn told Aleks. "I won't leave his side."

"And I'll follow you," Con told him.

"Take care of him," Aleks told Quinn, his voice desperate. Brogan's eyes had closed but he was comfortable and the antidote was hopefully working to clear the poison from his system.

"On my life," Quinn promised. Aleks watched the EMTs load Brogan into the ambulance, watched Quinn climb in after him and the doors close and the sirens blare before driving away.

Only then did he turn away from the police officer, presenting his hands behind his back as the officer read him his rights.

Hours later, Aleks sat in another cage, interrogated for hours on end. Brogan and Harry were well-known in the community. Aleks had killed a well-known businessman (true) and it appeared he'd poisoned another one (not true but hell, the police were on a roll and even Aleks had to admit that he looked guilty as fuck).

He was treated like a criminal for sure. And the worst part was that no one would tell him how Brogan was doing.

"You tried to kill him—what do you care? Or is it about beating a double murder rap?" the detective demanded.

Aleks kept his mouth shut for everything, except alternating asking for a lawyer and about Brogan's condition The threats, the yelling, they couldn't touch him. He'd been to hell and back. Knew the terrain intimately.

Finally, they took him for a piss before putting him in a holding cell. He hesitated briefly before the guard pushed him in forcibly and clanked the door behind him. He refused to turn around and look at the bars, instead focusing on the wall in front of him. His fingers curled into fists as he recalled all the days and nights he'd punched the cinderblock, toughening up, trying not to have a panic attack.

He didn't care how strong someone was—years in a confined space would do it to the strongest of souls. But he forced himself to breathe—for Brogan. Brogan was safe. Brogan was innocent in all of this—and Aleks had taken care of Harry for him, for Berdy and Lola and Vann. For himself and all the men and women Harry had harmed over the years.

He wasn't the only one. Aleks knew he couldn't stop there, but he also knew that this was the most personal struggle. That he could handle whatever came his way, better and stronger.

Brogan, come on, be okay. Please.

It was dark when the bars slid open with a loud clank and the officer said, "You're being released."

Aleks was given his clothes and belongings back, told not to leave town. Aleks glanced at the clock and noted that they'd held him for over twenty hours. They'd held him here while Brogan was fighting for his life—because Aleks refused to believe anything else.

Con was there waiting, with a five o'clock shadow, obviously had camped out in the police station and probably was precariously close to getting thrown out. But it was the big, quiet man in the corner who caught his eye next.

Vann. Coming toward him as Aleks felt the overall shock of everything that had happened set in. Vann embraced him and, just like he'd done all those years ago, he took Aleks's arm and tugged him out of the fire.

Chapter Seventeen

"He's alive, but still unconscious. They had to flush the drugs. He's holding his own," Con told Aleks as the three men walked to Con's car. Aleks crawled into the backseat, needing more space than a front seat could give, and Vann had Con open all the car's windows and the sunroof as they drove toward the hospital.

Aleks didn't say a word, not until he heard the doctor repeat what Con had told him. Then he asked, "Can I see him?"

"Yes," the doctor said, and motioned to the nurse to open the door to the ICU. "One at a time, and not for long."

Aleks nodded, feeling numb as he entered the room and saw Brogan lying there, pale and unmoving. He walked up to the hospital bed and folded Brogan into his arms. Didn't give a shit about the tubes and machines. He just wanted Brogan to feel him. Life force was a powerful thing.

"Don't let him win, Brogan. Don't let him take another person from me. Not fucking fair." Aleks kissed the side of Brogan's neck. "I love you, Brogan. You need to pull out of this so I can tell you, face to face. Please."

The nurses let him stay with Brogan longer than they should've—Aleks knew that but it still wasn't long enough.

"We've got to take some blood and change out tubing. Then you can come back in," a young nurse promised him, her eyes serious and kind.

Aleks reluctantly let go of Brogan and walked into the hallway and into the small waiting area where Con, Quinn and Vann had camped out. All he said was, "Same," and Con and Quinn stood.

"We'll grab you guys something to eat," Quinn told him.

"He's strong. He'll come through just fine," Con added.

Vann just sat there on the couch and patted at the open space next to him. Aleks curled against him, the way they would when forced to share a cage. Nothing sexual, all comfort. And time began to pass in a blur. In between sleeping and reports from the doctors and being given food and drink and being allowed to visit Brogan—and being vaguely aware of an older woman he semi-recognized coming in to talk to the other guys while he dozed off from stress and exhaustion— the sun began to come up. And finally, the doctor woke him up by saying, "Brogan's awake—and he's asking for you."

Aleks entered, slightly hesitantly until he saw that Brogan's eyes were indeed open and looking at him. He walked right up to the bed and took Brogan's hand. "How're you feeling?"

"Like shit." Brogan's voice was rough and scratchy from the tube that had been down his throat. "But I'm okay. What about you?"

"I'm fine," he said automatically.

"We'll talk about that." Brogan smiled a little.

"Really, I'm okay. Con and Quinn are here. Vann too," Aleks told him.

"I want to see him." Brogan's eyes meant business. Aleks went out and motioned him inside, and none of the nurses seemed inclined to argue with the big man in the leather MC rocker.

Vann walked to the bed and after Aleks introduced them, Brogan said, "Thank you." Vann frowned and Brogan continued, "Thank you for pulling him out of the fire so I could find him again."

Aleks stared up at the ceiling, feeling his eyes well up and goddammit it, he did not bond. But he had, and it was too late to attempt to deny it. He put a hand on Brogan's.

"He saved me as much as I did him," Vann said gruffly.

"I'm sorry you both went through that. I'm sorry my family was a part of it. I'll make it up to Aleks."

"I know you will. Just be good to him. You were a victim too." Vann's voice rumbled through the room and the men shared a handshake before Vann hugged Aleks and said, "I'm going to head back. Keep me updated. And remember you're coming to meet Emme. Bring Brogan."

"I will," Aleks promised.

He turned back to Brogan, who moved over as best he could so Aleks could shove up next to him.

"I like these rings." Brogan traced them along Aleks's right pec, the same way he had so many times before. Brogan had honed in on them early on, although he'd never asked about them specifically. Aleks wasn't sure what he'd have said if Brogan had asked.

"Yeah, me too."

"It's a symbol of a Russian wedding ring. Past. Present. Future," Brogan whispered.

Aleks stared at him, surprised. "You've been researching Russian wedding rings."

"Russian traditions. But the rose gold ring's missing. Rose gold is the future."

It was missing—not filled in, just barely outlined, like the ghost of a future Aleks never thought he'd have. He bit his bottom lip and finally said, "For a long time, it was just past and present. The future was on hold."

"And now?"

"Now he's here." Aleks squeezed his hand. "So don't fucking die on me, okay?"

"Okay," Brogan breathed. "I think I might like one of those."

"A wedding ring?"

"One of those tattoos," Brogan said. "But I'd consider the actual ring too. Past. Present. Future. All precious. And we'll survive all of it."

"That we will," Aleks told him fiercely. Then he lay his head down on Brogan's chest, listening to the steady heartbeat, too full of emotion to talk anymore.

But Brogan had other plans. "I love you too, Aleks."

Aleks blinked but didn't look up. Because Brogan had said 'too.' That meant… "You heard me?"

"Yes."

Aleks felt Brogan's hand in his hair. "Good."

Things improved with Brogan quickly after that, although the doctors kept him in bed with various IVs and other monitors. Aleks wouldn't leave his side except to go to Brogan's to grab him clothes and grab himself a quick shower.

As Aleks returned and rounded the corner to Brogan's hospital room, he saw the older woman he remembered from the waiting room. It was Brogan's aunt and another older man, armed with a briefcase, coming out. Aleks wasn't sure Brogan's aunt knew who he was, but she was already walking in his direction.

He was prepared for anything—a cold shoulder, a sharp remark—but he got a small smile and a soft, "Are you Aleks?"

"Yes, ma'am," he said automatically.

She held her hand out. "I'm Brogan's Aunt Margaret. I'd like to thank you for saving him. My sister..." She put her hand on her chest and took a breath. "All I wanted to do was take care of him. He's so much like her."

"He's a good man."

"And so are you," she said firmly. "Everything is taken care of. I'm so sorry. If I'd known..."

"It's okay. But thank you."

She gazed at him. "I'm looking forward to getting to know you further, Aleks."

"Same."

She nodded and then she and the tall, suited man walked on.

Aleks went into Brogan's room and found him sitting up, staring out the window. He brightened immediately upon seeing Aleks. "Hey. I'm thinking about sneaking out—want to help?"

"Nice try. But I'll stay here with you."

Brogan nodded. "That'll do."

"I, ah, just met your aunt."

"Yeah, she and her lawyer came by to talk to me," Brogan affirmed. "Without my uncle."

Aleks sat on the end of Brogan's bed. "Did you…?"

"They know now. They didn't before yesterday," Brogan said shortly. "And my uncle? He knew the entire goddamned time."

Aleks went cold inside. "Brogan—"

Brogan shook his head hard. "Don't. It's okay. My aunt is leaving my uncle. She's not perfect herself but she's not like them. My uncle's resigning his position. It's not going to take his fortune away but he won't have control anymore."

"And you? Because you didn't want this."

Brogan stared at him. "But it's mine. My responsibility. And it's time I started using the money to make up for what Harry and my uncle did. It might be too late but—"

"It's never too late," Aleks told him quietly. "It took me a long time to get here, but I know that's true now."

Epilogue

Brogan had been released after ten days. Aleks had moved into his place to help Brogan, who was supposed to limit his activities until all his blood tests came back clean from the long-acting drugs.

He'd moved in, and never moved out.

"I'd thought about buying my own place, but I found a sugar daddy instead," Aleks told him with a smirk and a shrug.

Brogan just rolled his eyes and said, "You've definitely been hanging out with Con too much."

Now, Brogan was sprawled out, half naked, under him. On Aleks's tattoo table in the middle of Inked.

"First tattoo's a big deal," Aleks murmured as he held the gun, ready to freehand the rings on Brogan's skin. His own ring tattoo had been finished last night by Quinn as Brogan watched, and now Brogan glanced at the healing tattoo and then Aleks's eyes.

"First and only."

"That's what they all say," Aleks said.

Brogan smiled and touched Aleks's hand. "I mean it."

Aleks smiled back. "I know you do."

HOLD THE LINE

INKED 1

On sale now!

*Holding on loosely has never been
such a challenge...*

What happens when a tattoo artist and a Delta Force soldier
keep a promise and take a cross-country trip together? Quinn
and Con are about to finally meet and find out.

Quinn thinks he's the responsible one, but he quickly learns
that he needs to loosen up if he's got any shot of holding onto
Con.

*(*This novella is now available as a standalone, but was
previously published in the Danger Zone Anthology, with all
proceeds going to Hope For the Warrior.)*

ALSO BY SE JAKES

Men of Honor Series
BOUND BY HONOR
BOUND BY LAW
TIES THAT BIND
BOUND BY DANGER
BOUND FOR KEEPS
BOUND TO BREAK

Phoenix, Inc. Series
NO BOUNDARIES

Inked Series
HOLD THE LINE
THIRDS

EE LTD. Universe
FREE FALLING

Hell or High Water Series
CATCH A GHOST
LONG TIME GONE
DAYLIGHT AGAIN
NOT FADE AWAY
IF I EVER *(forthcoming)*

Dirty Deeds Series
DIRTY DEEDS

Havoc MC Series
RUNNING WILD

Bluewater Bay (multi-author series)
NO EASY WAY (novella) in the *LIGHTS, CAMERA, ACTION* Anthology

WRITING AS
STEPHANIE TYLER

Shelter Series
SHELTER ME
PIECES OF ME (coming Fall 2016)

Mirror Series
MIRROR ME
RULE OF THIRDS
WALK IN MY SHADOW
DOUBLE BLIND (coming 2017)

Skulls Creek MC Series
VIPERS RUN
VIPERS RULE

Section 8 Series
SURRENDER
UNBREAKABLE
FRAGMENTED

Defiance Series
DEFIANCE
REDEMPTION
SALVATION
TEMPERANCE

Dire Wolves Series
DIRE WARNING (prequel novella)
DIRE NEEDS
DIRE WANTS
DIRE DESIRES

Shadow Force Series
LIE WITH ME
PROMISES IN THE DARK
IN THE AIR TONIGHT
NIGHT MOVES
LONELY IS THE NIGHT

Hold Series
HARD TO HOLD
TOO HOT TO HOLD
HOLD ON TIGHT
HOLDING ON (novella)

Hot Nights, Dark Desires Anthology
NIGHT VISION (novella)

Harlequin Blaze
COMING UNDONE
RISKING IT ALL
BEYOND HIS CONTROL

WRITING AS SYDNEY CROFT

ACRO Series
RIDING THE STORM
UNLEASHING THE STORM
SEDUCED BY THE STORM
TAMING THE FIRE
TEMPTING THE FIRE
TAKEN BY FIRE
THREE THE HARD WAy (novella)

Hot Nights, Dark Desires Anthology
SHADOW PLAY (novella)

ABOUT THE AUTHOR

SE JAKES is the pen name for *New York Times* bestselling author Stephanie Tyler, and half the co-writing team of Sydney Croft. First published in 2011, SE Jakes has quickly risen to be a bestselling author in the LGBT romance genre, as well as a fan favorite. Her books are frequently highlighted in *USA Today* and have been reviewed by *Library Journal* and *RT Books Magazine*. She's been nominated by several sites for Favorite M/M author and has finaled in the Goodreads M/M Romance Readers Choice Awards in 7 categories. She's a hybrid author who writes for Riptide Publishing and Samhain Publishing, and she indie publishes as well.

STEPHANIE TYLER is the *New York Times* bestselling author of romance novels spanning multiple genres, including Romantic Suspense, New Adult, Paranormal Romance and Contemporary Romance. She's a hybrid author who writes for multiple publishers, including Random House, NAL/Penguin, Harlequin, Carina Press, Mammoth Books, Belle Books and Samhain Publishing, as well as Riptide (as SE Jakes) and indie publishing. Her books have been translated into half a dozen languages, nominated for an RT Readers' Choice Award and garnered top picks from *RT Book Magazine* as well as starred reviews from *Publishers Weekly*. She's a frequent workshop presenter and has contributed stories for anthologies for charities, including **SEAL of My Dreams**, which has raised over 150K for the Veterans Medical Association.

SYDNEY CROFT is the alter ego of Stephanie Tyler and Larissa Ione, two *New York Times* bestselling authors who blend their very different writing interests into adventurous tales of erotic paranormal fiction. Together, they developed a world where people with extraordinary abilities, like the power to control storms, could live and work with others like them. The series has been described as "Erotica meets the X-Men," and is unique in its own "erotic superhero romance" niche. Larissa and Stephanie live in different states and communicate almost entirely through email, though they often get together for conferences and book signings.